QUEER EYE FOR THE SUPER GUY

Solar System Services, Inc.
Alone Is Not Lonely
Halloween Harvest ("A Place at the Table")

Millersburg Magick Mysteries
Spells and Sleuths
Fae and Felonies
Magick and Murder

Soccer Moms of the Apocalypse
Pestilence in Pumpkin Spice
Famine In French Vanilla
War in White Chocolate
Death in Double Mocha

Miscellaneous
Sword and Sorceress 31 ("Pig-Headed")
Sword and Sorceress 32 ("Unexpected")
Practical Witches
Revenge Served Hot
The Yule Switch
Chocolate for Dinner
Silver Shoes and Pigs' Ears

For updates, news, and giveaways, join Suzan's mailing list or visit her website at www.suzanharden.com. You can also check her out on Facebook @SuzanHardenWriter.

Queer Eye

for the

Super Guy

888-555-HERO #11

Suzan Harden

This is a work of fiction. All characters, organizations and events in this story are products of the author's imagination and are not to be construed as real. Any resemblance to persons, living or dead, is entirely coincidental.

QUEER EYE FOR THE SUPER GUY
(888-555-HERO #11)

ISBN-13 - 978-1-64918-036-0

Published by Angry Sheep Publishing
Findlay, Ohio

Interior Design by JW Manus
Cover Design by For the Muse Design

*For Hot Chocolate, RuPaul, and all the queens who
have entertained and inspired me over the years,
thanks for the glitter and glam!*

CHAPTER 1

Jeremy Harkness examined the business plan his husband Leonardo had set on the counter while he chopped mushrooms for their breakfast omelets. The idea was sound, but . . .

He set aside the knife and looked up at Leonardo who perched on a stool on the opposite side of their kitchen island. "But why, darling?"

"Why, what?" Leonardo frowned.

"I don't understand why you'd want to design for the hoi polloi, baby doll," Jeremy answered.

"The general public is not the hoi polloi, and no offense—" Leonardo hesitated a moment before he blurted, "I want a little something to call my own. I hate feeling like I'm riding on your dress train."

"You're not—" Jeremy started to protest.

"If we don't promote Elaine, she's going to leave to start her own salon." Leonardo pantomimed trading one thing for another. "Besides Rey already set aside space for us in the new Canyon Block shopping complex."

Rey Garcia, AKA the superhero Black Falcon, was generous to a fault. He, or rather his attorneys, finally managed to close on the city block that had housed Canyon Industries, Canyon Pointe's largest employer until the company collapsed nearly three decades ago. Rey was making sure the homeless folks he knew had jobs and places to live since he had been one of them not so long ago.

Not to mention Rey made Jeremy's foster sister Aisha so damn happy. It was hard to hate the man for being good-looking and a total sweetheart, too.

"And I've already got my first client," Leonardo added. "Mother Defiant asked me to design her wedding dress."

"She can be such a pain," Jeremy warned.

"Actually, she's lightened up quite a bit since she and Blue Racer moved in together."

Jeremy nodded. "All right. We can withdraw the cash from one of our money market funds—"

"No." Leonardo held up his right palm. "I've already set aside the capital I will need, and Mother Defiant already gave me a down payment on her wedding dress."

"Leonardo Park Harkness!" Jeremy laid his palm on his chest. "You have secret money I don't know about?"

"Quit being a drama queen." Leonardo scowled. "I've been squirreling away money in my fun account for years."

Jeremy sighed and bit his lower lip. He'd been the one to insist they have separate accounts for their own personal use so neither of them had to justify such spending to the other spouse. His bio parents had some rather nasty fights over Dad's race track betting and Mom's shoe shopping before they tossed Jeremy out of the house. He sighed. The 'rents probably still had those same fights.

Assuming they were still together. Jeremy hadn't bothered checking up on them.

"Don't give me the sigh of disbelief," Leonardo said crossly.

Jeremy leaned his elbows on the counter and took Leonardo's hands in his. "It was the sigh of self-disgust that I was on the verge of acting like my bio 'rents. And for that, I sincerely apologize, my love."

Leonardo flashed a sweet smile. "All's forgiven." He leaned closer and pecked Jeremy on the lips.

"Can I see some of your designs?" Jeremy asked when they parted.

"Not yet," Leonardo said.

A little twinge of anxiety raced along Jeremy's nerves. He knew it was a stupid reaction to what Ryan had done to him fifteen years ago. And it definitely wasn't fair to compare that asshole to Leonardo.

"I'm actually working with Susan Kennedy," Leonardo continued. "She's been designing jewelry on the side."

"She is?" Jeremy blinked, but he didn't know why he was surprised. His foster sisters' law partner was a fountain of odd talents. "Wait a minute! Was she where you came up with the idea for the earring comms for the supers who wear jewelry?"

Leonardo nodded. "I said one set she showed me was big enough to hide Timmy's equipment, and we got to talking."

Jeremy was a big enough queen to admit his feelings were hurt, but he also wanted his husband to be happy. "Just make sure you have someone look over any partnership papers before you sign anything."

Leonardo's eyes widened. "Do you really think Susan would screw me over?"

Jeremy chuckled. "Only if she really wants Harri and Aisha to pound the crap out of her. But this is your baby, and I'll stay out of your way, muffin."

His phone chose that moment to dance along the surface of the island's granite countertop to the tune of Helen Reddy's "I Am Woman." Even odder was the caller ID showed Melanie's personal number, not their alter ego, Ultramegaperson.

He tapped the answer icon. "What's up, doll?"

"I have a personal question for you and a request." The throaty voice of the world's most powerful super purred through the receiver. "Remember that producer Dale I've been dating?"

"You've mentioned him." Jeremy grabbed his phone and stepped back to lean against the sink counter. Leonardo pulled the cutting board towards himself and started mincing the garlic.

"He wants to know if my designer would like to be involved in a nationally televised reality show where twelve designers for superheroes would compete to dress twelve brand-new supers."

"Mel, you know I like my privacy when it comes to designing supersuits," Jeremy said.

"Which is the reason I'm calling you instead of my boyfriend Dale calling you." Mel gave an exaggerated sigh. "You know I'd be the last person on the planet to out your secret designing skills, but since you design for a large number of other heroes, he really wants you to participate in his show."

"What's the catch?" Jeremy said.

"One of the twelve people the contestants will be designing for is a supervillain."

CHAPTER 2

Before Harri went downstairs to her law office, she knocked on the door of Aisha's loft. She didn't mind Molly Reinhold loftsitting. It was the other resident that bothered her.

When no one answered, Harri punched in the keycode. The pad flashed green, and she rolled back the door. To her left, Aisha's dining table had been commandeered by a sewing machine, loads of fabric, and several giant spools of thread. A dressmaker's dummy stood guard over the organized chaos. To her right came Molly and Monica Reinhold's voices. It sounded like another mother/daughter squabble. Harri locked the door and headed down the hall.

"Mom, you've got to eat something." Molly wasn't whining, but there was a subsonic burr in her voice that grated on Harri's nerves. It also meant the superhero known as Nix was about to lose her temper.

"I didn't ask for you to babysit me," Monica snarled.

"Would you like to stay at Grandma's?" Molly shot back.

Whatever Monica was about to say to her daughter was silenced with the snap of her teeth at Harri's appearance in the doorway to Aisha's spare bedroom. The normally immaculate supervillain Miss Purrception lay limply in the twin bed like a rag doll that had been run over a few times by Julio and his garbage truck.

"How are you feeling today?" Harri asked.

"I'm just peachy, counselor," Monica sneered. She pushed

herself up, but her wince indicated she still wasn't mending like she should.

"That's good because I have a headache." Molly stormed past Harri and out of the bedroom.

"What do you want?" Monica pushed her dark, dirty locks out of her face. Flecks of silver and white shone along her scalp. The vain supervillian had been on the run at least a month if she hadn't bothered touching up her roots. She hadn't given anyone much more information other than her own mother Margaret Reinhold, AKA esteemed superhero Rue Liberty, had shot Monica after Rue had killed Byron Trubble, the former head of the black ops organization known as Corvus.

Harri leaned against the doorjamb, crossed her arms, and watched her former client. Her own emerging gray hadn't bothered her. She let Jeremy or Leo color her damn hair every six weeks just to get them to shut up about it.

"Molly's right," she said. "You need to eat."

"So you can send me back to Mauvaises?" Monica mocked.

"We both know you'll be dead within a week if I do that." Harri sighed. "But if you don't eat and do your physical therapy, you'll never be able to escape the Lechuza Building and rub it in Tim's face."

"Sometimes, I don't know whose side you're on," Monica spat.

"That makes us even since I'm never sure which way you'll jump in a given situation," Harri responded.

"Then what do you want?" Monica leaned back wearily on her pillows.

"Would you happen to have any more bullets like the ones you were shot with?"

"Just the ones Serena pulled out of my chest and gut." Monica's eyes narrowed. "Why?"

"They were designed to fragment upon impact—"

"And tear up the target." Monica sighed. "Those things are available at any ammo store in the U.S."

"Tim thinks there was something inside the ones you were shot with," Harri said. "Something that's impeding your super healing ability. You should have been up and around—"

"And escaping?" The smile on Monica's face was only a whisper of her usual sly smirk.

"At least five days ago," Harri finished. "That's accounting for both the damage and Serena's initial attempt to heal you."

The physician's assistant at the end of the block had nearly burned out her own superpower in trying to help Monica. Harri wondered if the supervillain even appreciated what Serena had done for her.

"All I wanted from the kid was a patch job and enough pain-killers to get me down to Mexico." Monica wouldn't look at Harri anymore. Instead, she stared at the steel rafters overhead. "I didn't ask her to heal me. Or to call O'Brien."

Doctor Hannah O'Brien ran the neighborhood clinic where Serena worked. Both Harri and Rey made regular donations to keep the clinic open since most of the folks in the Canyon Block didn't have health insurance. If they could only get a dentist on this side of town . . .

"I'm the one who called O'Brien if you want to get pissy," Harri said dryly. "And if Rue wanted you dead, she would've shot you in the head, then decapitated you."

"She tried the head shot." Monica lifted a section of lank hair by her left temple. What looked like a fresh burn scarred her scalp. "I got lucky, or she's getting old. Either way, she missed."

Barely, but Harri kept that opinion to herself. "If Rue has developed bullets that can hurt supers like you—"

"Of course, she has." Monica squeezed her eyes shut. "It's always been about power for her. She's got to be top dog."

Her act almost made Harri feel sorry for the woman. Unfortunately, Monica had lied too many times for Harri to ever trust her again.

"Like I said before," Harri said. "Cut a deal with the FBI. Consuelo has cleaned up her office—"

A sharp bark of laughter erupted from Monica that led to a coughing fit. Harri didn't try to assist the supervillain. Not that she didn't have any compassion for the injured woman, but she knew Monica wouldn't respect her attempt if she did.

When Monica's fit died and she collapsed back on her pillows, Harri said, "So you'd rather cough out a lung, then to help us stop your mother?"

"Tell Tim, there's modified bullets in one of my old safe houses." Monica smirked. "The first one I let him see."

Harri wanted to beat the expression off the supervillain's mug. She didn't have to ask why Monica left the bullets in that particular place. It was her little dig that she had her claws in Harri's husband long before they got married.

"Thank you for your assistance," Harri said. "Are there any new booby-traps he doesn't know about?"

"No," Monica said. "But he might want to take Steve with him. Tim's getting a little slow in his old age." Rey's twin brother had the same power set as him, but Steve had no interest in joining the underwear brigade. Monica's jibe may sting Tim's ego, but for safety's sake, Harri would insist he take Steve with him anyway.

"So are you if a senior citizen got the drop on you, Miss Purrception." Harri pivoted and strode out of Aisha's spare bedroom before she said or did something she'd really regret.

CHAPTER 3

"Are you friggin' kidding me?" Jeremy shouted. "I will not have a supervillian wearing one of my creations!"

Leonardo frowned and laid aside the knife. Well out of Jeremy's reach.

"No, no, no," Mel replied. "Dale wants you to be one of the judges, not one of the designer contestants."

If Mel wasn't totally immune to the effects of any and all drugs, Jeremy would suspect they were high on something.

"This Dale better be worth it in bed," he grumbled.

"Oh, he is." Mel laughed. "Why do you think I'm just getting home?"

"Let me talk it over with Leonardo and call you back."

"Can I have Dale's assistant send the contracts to Winters and Franklin for their review?"

"That's awfully presumptuous of you," Jeremy retorted.

"Puh-leease. We both know you won't sign a damn thing without your foster sisters' input."

Jeremy looked at Leonardo who wore a shit-eating grin. Oh, he was definitely going to hear about this over breakfast. "All right, e-mail the contracts to Harri. But this is not a yes by any means, Mel."

"Of course. Talk to you later." Mel made kissy noises before they ended the call.

Jeremy glared at Leonardo. "What are you laughing about?"

"We both know if the money's right, you're going to do it."

"Did you know about this show Mel's boyfriend is making?" Jeremy laid his phone on the counter before he pulled out the carton of eggs from the refrigerator.

"There's been rumors in the gossip rags that TV wunderkind Dale Bernhardt has signed a producing deal with the ABS network." Leonardo shrugged and popped a mushroom slice in his mouth. "The execs want a show to compete with the reality series on their rivals. Between cable and streaming, they are hemorrhaging money like crazy."

"You mean reality shows are cheap." Jeremy cracked two eggs into his mixing bowl, added two tablespoons of water, and whisked everything until it was evenly smooth and yellow. Did he really want to out himself? Mel didn't care if they were outed or not. Very little could hurt them. Plus, they always kept their relationships casual. Jeremy, on the other hand, had Leonardo, his foster sibs, and his foster parents to worry about being used against him.

Jeremy cut a pat of butter into the small non-stick skillet and turned on the heat. He had some issues with some supervillains when he first started designing for supers. If it weren't for Mel, he'd be dead. But the odd thing was Mel never held it over his head when they asked for a favor.

"It would mean living out on the West Coast for a few months," Jeremy murmured.

"What's the point of having your clients train the local Alphabets to take care of themselves if you can't stop being a mother hen?" Leonardo asked while he diced the onions.

"Your parents accepted you for what you are, babykins."

"Being gay, yes. Marrying you, yes, though Mom sides with Betty about us eloping. But my parents didn't agree with a lot of other stuff in my life."

"That's because you can freaking do calculus in your head.

You should be teaching at MIT." Jeremy sobered and swirled the melting butter around in the pan. "You have no idea what it's like to live on the streets."

"The only reason you do is because you let your pride get in the way," Leonardo responded gently. "I know damn well once Harri and Aisha found out what had happened between you and your parents, they talked Betty and Marvin into helping you."

Jeremy shuddered. If it weren't for Aisha's parents taking him in along with Harri—well, he'd come pretty damn close to prostitution in order to eat. On the other hand, Leonardo was right. He'd lived on the streets out of a misplaced sense of pride.

"A couple of months in California would be a perfect opportunity to see how Elaine can handle the salon," Leonardo continued. "We get a furnished apartment. I can take my laptop and work on my designs while you're at the studio."

"You're jumping way ahead here." Jeremy poured the eggs into the bubbling butter. "I haven't agreed to a damn thing yet. But you're right about giving Elaine a probationary period as manager." He added the onions, garlic, mushrooms, and shredded Swiss cheese.

"You want me to talk to her?" Leonardo rose to refill his coffee cup.

Jeremy considered the matter. "When is your first appointment today?"

"I'm booked from one to nine." Leonardo set his filled cup on the breakfast bar and reached for Jeremy's mug.

"Let's go in early and take her out to lunch," Jeremy suggested.

Leonardo paused and looked at him. "Mabel Longwood is my first client."

"She can handle it if you're late." He shook his head. "You can't let people like Mabel run roughshod over you."

"Oh, please, darling." Leonardo glared at him. "You let her run over you when she was your client, too."

"And then, I did the smart thing and dumped her on the cute, naïve, new stylist who joined my salon." Jeremy smirked while he flipped the omelet in the pan.

"You are evil." Leonardo laughed and shook his head. "It's a wonder you didn't become a supervillain."

"And have a certain foster sister beat the crap out of me if I did?" Jeremy slid the finished omelet onto one of the waiting plates and handed it to his husband. "No, thank you."

"I admit Harri is a full of bark—" Leonardo said.

"Harri would only yell at me. I wasn't referring to her." Jeremy dropped another pat of butter in the omelet pan and cracked two more eggs in the mixing bowl.

"Aisha would only resort to fisticuffs if—"

"Not her either. She'd give me the same disappointed parent look Marvin would have." Jeremy whipped the eggs with two tablespoons of water.

"LaShun?" Leonardo wore a confused expression. "Wouldn't she break a nail?"

"Do not underestimate her, darling." Jeremy poured the egg mixture into the bubbling butter. The liquid hissed and steamed. "When we were kids, she towed Mama Betty's line, and she made sure the rest of us did, too. And that was long before Betty and Marvin let Harri and me move in with the Franklin clan."

Leonardo giggled. "What would LaShun do?"

"Pull my hair." Jeremy ran a hand over his locks. "Sit on me, or dig those damn claws of hers into very sensitive flesh as a last resort."

Leonardo winced in sympathetic pain. "What did you do for LaShun to resort to the third option?"

"I used her makeup without permission." Jeremy smiled at

the memory while he added fillings to his omelet. "But the next day she took me to Arrow's and helped me select my own makeup while she lectured me on not sharing products because of germs. She even pitched in her own allowance to pay for everything and gave me my first lesson on proper application."

"And here, I thought she had no heart." Leonardo chuckled.

"She and Betty are a lot alike." Jeremy flipped his omelet in half. "In a way, they care too much. Then, there's the perfectionistic streak. Eat your omelet before it gets cold. And please call Elaine after breakfast so she doesn't have lunch without us."

"And what will you be doing?"

Jeremy slid his omelet onto his own plate. "I need to call my attorney to draw up Elaine's paperwork and consult with her about the contracts Mel's boyfriend will be sending to her."

As he dug into his breakfast, he wondered if it would really be worth his time to participate in Dale Bernhardt's reality show. Because the idea of an unknown supervillain involved worried him to no end.

CHAPTER 4

Harri sipped her cinnamon coffee and stared at the e-mail she just received from Dale Bernhardt's assistant Keisha. She'd heard of Hollywood's latest "it" producer, but the email made no sense. Keisha referred to Ultramegaperson's supersuit designer, but she didn't mention the person by name. Harri couldn't imagine Jeremy breaking his silence over that particular side hustle.

Was this Keisha really Bernhardt's assistant? If she was, how did Bernhardt know Harri had been representing Jeremy's business interests? Surely, Ultramegaperson hadn't outed Jeremy.

Had they?

Harri reached for the intercom to get her IT guru Arthur Drallhickey to trace the email when the device buzzed. She punched the button. "Yes?"

"You busy?" Janna Gomez asked. The firm's morning receptionist and all-around Girl Friday was pretty good about screening calls when Harri was neck deep in work.

As she usually was these days with Aisha living in Paris for the rest of the year.

"It's Jeremy about some contract that was supposed to be forwarded to you," Janna added.

"Put him through." Harri picked up the handset before the first ring completed. "Hey, sister dearest. Give me some warning before you have someone send me attachments to emails. That's a good way to infect the firm's computers."

"Dale already sent you the paperwork?" Jeremy sounded surprised. "I didn't expect him to move that fast. Ultramegaperson called me a half hour ago while I was making breakfast."

Harri leaned back in her office chair. "Ultra called you? Jaye, why don't you start from the beginning?"

He filled her in on his conversation with Ultramegaperson this morning, including his agreement to let Bernhardt send the initial paperwork to Harri.

"A reality show?" She reached for her coffee. "Are you sure this is worth outing yourself over?"

"No, but I trust you to make sure this deal is worth outing myself over."

"Has Bernhardt sent you copies of this deal?" she asked.

"I trust Mel not to name me," Jeremy said. "All Bernhardt knows is Ultramegaperson uses the same law firm as the person who designs their supersuits."

"Okay, let's open up this puppy and see what Mr. Hollywood is offering my favorite sister."

Jeremy snorted. "I'm only your favorite right now because Aisha's in Paris."

"Is it okay if I run this past her tomorrow morning?" Harri asked.

"What about Susan? You know, your other partner?" Jeremy sniped. "Or are you still holding a grudge?"

Harri clenched her teeth. Of course he'd bring up the fight she had with Susan a couple of weeks ago. She'd apologized to her partner, but things were still a little tense in the firm.

Especially after Harri found out the rest of the staff, including her own damn husband, sided with the newest partner.

"I was planning to have her look over the offer this afternoon," Harri shot back. "If that's okay, Your Majesty."

"The more the merrier," he said.

Harri opened the attachment. The cover letter laid out the basic offer, which made her whistle.

"Don't leave me hanging, Harri!"

"Bernhardt wants you as the main judge of the show." She named the number of zeroes after the first number.

Jeremy whooped. "Are you shitting me?"

"Nope. He's also already lined up the tax credits to film the series here in Canyon Pointe."

"What do you mean film in Canyon Pointe?" Suspicion dripped from Jeremy's voice.

She couldn't blame him. Between normal everyday bigots and the illegal black-op organization known as Corvus, there were many reasons for his insane desire for personal privacy.

"According to this, he wants to complete the lineup of judges and contestants before he approaches famous Canyon Pointe drag queen Lady Jaye about using her nightclub for filming." Harri laughed. "This is too funny to be true. You might want to do this whole thing as Lady Jaye."

"It's not funny," Jeremy snapped.

"Actually, it might work better," she said. "Few people outside of your lost boys and the family know Lady Jaye's real identity. And you know the staff at the club will make sure no one finds out."

"And you know Coco will go absolutely Miss Purrception on me if I agree to the show filming at the club," Jeremy protested. He could already hear his manager for the Revue going absolutely apeshit about disrupting her routine. "Not to mention security issues if Bernhardt is crazy enough to really have a supervillain as a contestant. Or have you not read that far yet?"

Harri ignored Jeremy while she scanned the second page of the proposal, and when she reached the list of pending judges, her blood ran cold. "Oh, shit."

"What's wrong, hun?"

"One of the pending judges is Nix."

CHAPTER 5

Jeremy whistled. "I take it the kid hasn't said anything to you about the show."

"She has the right to have additional representation." But there was an edge to his foster sister's tone.

"Or maybe she and Aisha are talking again?" Jeremy ventured. "That would be a plus."

Molly had been rather put out Aisha and Rey hadn't asked her to go to Paris with them as Mitch's nanny. In fact, the Franklin-Garcias had tried to encourage Molly to go to school and do something with her life than just superheroing. Especially since her twin sister had moved out of their grandmother's house and was attending classes at a local automotive servicing school.

"Aisha would have said something to me if that were the case," Harri murmured.

"Oh, geez, woman! Are you still jealous Aisha has the people skills?" Jeremy complained. Harri was a brilliant attorney and a good person, but her E.Q. was practically nonexistent.

"No, it's . . ." Slurping came over the receiver. "I trust Ultra to look out for themselves. Molly can be a little naïve."

He knew exactly where Harri was going with this, and he didn't like it. Not one bit.

"No, no, no. I revamped her costume and look. I am not going to babysit Nix for you."

"She's not going to listen to me if I try to talk her out of joining this reality show," she said.

Jeremy pinched the bridge of his nose. "Sweetie, cut Nix a break. Her whole life has revolved around rebelling against female authority figures."

"That's because her mom abandoned her," Harri snapped.

"Oh, and Rue Liberty's overprotectiveness had nothing to do with it?" Jeremy immediately regretted his mocking tone. At least, Rue fought for her granddaughters. None of his extended family would have anything to do with him after his parents kicked him out.

"I'm sorry," he said. "But make sure she's actually going to be a judge on this show before you freak out. Producers sometimes dangle big names to land other suckers, and Nix is a big name thanks to you and Aisha."

"You're not going to take any responsibility?" Harri mocked.

"I was trying to be a little gracious here," he shot back.

"All right, all right." Harri's sigh whistled over the receiver. "Let me talk to Molly and have Susan and Aisha look over your contract."

"And I want more money if I have to babysit Screaming Orgasm again." Jeremy grinned at Harri's groan of despair. She and Aisha worked hard to convince Molly the moniker she chose to piss off her grandmother wasn't doing the kid any favors.

"Fine." Harri chuckled. "Then I'm claiming one of the dinners at La Churro's you owe me for tonight."

"You have to pay for your own husband this time," he shot back, though he knew he'd pay so Leonardo didn't give him grief about being cheap. Besides, he rather liked lording it over Harri's ex-billionaire husband.

"Fine. How's seven sound?"

"Don't let me forget some takeout for my own husband. He's stuck at the salon until closing."

"I'll leave mine at home, and if I have news, I can pick up dinner as a business expense," Harri said.

Jeremy laughed. "You're incorrigible, sister of mine. I'll see you at seven." He pushed back from his desk, grabbed his coffee cup, and headed for the kitchen.

Leonardo sat on a stool, bent over the breakfast island, and was very intent on whatever he was doing. The rough scratching of pencil on paper came from the same direction.

Jeremy brushed back his husband's electric blue-highlighted hair and kissed his neck.

Leonardo jumped and slammed his notebook shut. "Quit trying to sneak a peek!"

"I wasn't. I swear." Jeremy circled the island and reached for the coffee pot. "What did Elaine say?"

"About freakin' time."

Jeremy paused in pouring his coffee and eyed Leonardo. "Excuse me?"

"That was a direct quote." Leonardo grinned. "I told you she needed to be promoted."

Jeremy leaned his elbows on the granite surface of the island. "Maybe I didn't want to replace my one and only."

Leonardo narrowed his eyes. "The only time I'd object to being replaced is in your bed, lover boy."

"I'd never dream of anyone else with me between the sheets." Jeremy took Leonardo's hand in his and kissed the back. "When I said forever, I meant it, baby doll. By the way, what do you want me to bring you from La Churro's?"

Leonardo laughed. "Harri's collecting on her bet again, isn't she?"

"It depends on if she has news about the TV deal for me by seven."

"I was teasing this morning," Leonardo said. "Are you really going to do this? Months in California?"

"Bernhardt let a few things slip in his email to Harri." Jeremy repeated the tidbits his sister found in the first two pages.

Leonardo whistled. "I admit I feel better about shooting the series here, but Bernhardt really has no idea that you and Lady Jaye are the same person?"

"Oh, I'm sure he's done his research, all right." Jeremy shook his head. "He probably knows Jeremy Harkness is Lady Jaye, but he doesn't know Jeremy Harkness is Mel's designer. Yet."

Leonardo frowned. "Are you sure this is a good idea?"

"I don't like the idea of a supervillain finding out who I am." Jeremy tapped his fingers on the countertop. "If one of those bozos decides I'm worth kidnapping, or worse goes after you or the sibs, to try to force me to give up my client list—"

Leonardo exhaled gustily. "But Harri wants you to keep an eye on Molly if she really is a judge, doesn't she?"

"The kid is sweet, but there's a reason the other Canyon Pointe supers make sure she's teamed up with one of them when stuff happens in the city." Jeremy rolled his eyes.

"I'm sorry about the money crack I made earlier," Leonardo said. "I know you wouldn't risk me or your foster family."

"It's okay." Jeremy leaned across the island and kissed his husband. Maybe they were still in the throes of being newlyweds, but he was so damn lucky to have Leonardo in his life. "You're right. I have been obsessed with money the last twenty years. I need to get over myself."

"But you're still going to do this reality show to make sure Molly doesn't get in trouble, aren't you?" Leonardo asked.

"I won't if you tell me no, darling," Jeremy replied.

Leonardo shook his head. "I'm not going to tell you what to do."

"But—" Jeremy drawled.

"I know you'll do the right thing." Leonardo made shooing motions with both hands. "And Harri's right. Someone needs to watch that girl. Now, go change so we can have lunch with Elaine."

"Yes, ma'am." Jeremy winked before he strolled to their bedroom. Leonardo was right. He would do the right thing, and the right thing was to keep the naïve Nix from getting herself into big trouble.

CHAPTER 6

A knock on Harri's office door interrupted her and Susan while they ripped through the provisional contract Dale Bernhardt's assistant had emailed.

Come in," Harri yelled.

Molly poked her head around the edge of the door. "Oh, you guys are busy. I can come back."

"What did your mother do this time?" Susan asked.

Molly paused. "It's not her. This time."

"Then come on in." Harri waved the young super into the office. "We could use a break."

"Well—" Molly stepped inside and closed the office door. A sheaf of papers were in her hand. "This is a matter for my lawyers."

She crossed the room and split her sheaf in two before she handed each portion to each attorney. "Before you start yelling at me, I haven't signed anything. I've been invited to be a judge on a new reality series, but I told the producer I would have to have the offer reviewed by my attorney before I could give him an answer."

The letterhead was Dale Bernhardt's production company as Harri expected. The surprising part was Molly's notes in the margins.

"When did you get this?" Susan asked.

"Yesterday." Molly walked over to one of Harri's couches and perched on the edge. "I did as you guys and Aisha taught me. I listened to Dale's pitch before I said he needed to send me a copy of the paperwork for you guys."

Harri looked up from Nix's initial offer. "Why not have it sent directly to us?"

Molly winced. "Please don't be mad. I've been helping Patty with LSAT flashcards while Arthur watches Grace." Patty Ames, the firm's paralegal, was scheduled to take the April test. She wasn't happy with her October score on the law school entrance exam. Luckily, she had time to retake the test before admissions closed at the university.

Panic flashed through Harri. "You've been leaving your mother alone?"

"Hell, no," Molly bit out. "Patty comes up to Aisha's loft. And Monica Reinhold is not my mom. She's a supervillain witness to a murder who I'm guarding." She slashed her hand through the air. "That's the extent of our relationship."

Harri leaned her elbow on her desk as she regarded the superhero. "Who's with her right now?"

Molly almost pouted over the question about her common sense, but she regained control of her emotions. "Steve's watching her while I'm down here with you."

Harri relaxed a little bit. "Thank you, Molly. I don't like having Monica here anymore than you do, but we don't have any place more secure where we can keep her. I don't want her to end up dead."

"Are you ever going to tell me who shot her?" Molly asked.

"For your own safety, no." Harri waited for an explosion from the younger woman.

"I figured out on my own it's the same person who murdered Trubble." Molly's eyes glittered more than usual. She was pissed as hell about being kept in the dark.

Harri got up from her chair, walked over to the couch, and sat next to the superhero. "Which is exactly why I'm not telling you. I couldn't handle it if the killer came after you."

"May I continue?" Molly's frosty tone indicated she wasn't going to accept Harri's reasons for keeping quiet regarding her mother's assailant.

But damn. It was going to kill the kid to learn her grandmother had secretly gone to the dark side years ago when Molly did learn the truth.

"Please do," Susan said as she took a seat on the second couch. From the mischievous expression on her face, Harri was going to get an earful when Molly left the office.

"I read the offer letter and the contract—" Molly held up the palm of her right hand briefly. "Before you start chewing me a new one, I highlighted the parts I didn't understand. But I did some research on the numbers some of these other reality shows bring in. With certain supers and designers as judges, potential new supers looking to build their fan base, and Dale Bernhardt's name on the project, he can do a lot better on the offer he sent me."

Molly grinned and lowered her hand. "Plus, it broke on the tabloids this morning Dale and Ultramegaperson are an item."

Harri flopped against the back of the couch and rubbed her temples. "How fucking convenient!"

"Harri!" Susan snapped. "We do not use that kind of language in regard to our clients." From the hot pink flushing Susan's face, Harri needed to do some serious backpedaling.

"I'm sorry to both of you." Harri straightened. "I just thought Ultra had more sense—"

"Than I do," Molly retorted.

"Molly, Bernhardt's pulled three of Winters and Franklin's clients into this program of his," Susan said. "Representing you in this matter may be a moot point."

The superhero turned to Harri. "You'd chose one of the other clients over me? I was one of the first—"

"Slow down." Harri grabbed Molly's closest flailing hand before she accidentally poked out Harri's eye with her wickedly sharp, glittery nails. "We need to talk to the others."

"But according to the State of Mojave's Revised Civil Code, if we all agree to Winters and Franklin representing us, you can still do it," Molly said with a hopeful expression on her face.

"But that means we can't keep secrets," Susan added. "You're all going to know how much each of you makes plus any perks."

Molly nodded. "I get it. To give you a heads-up, Dale got some tax breaks to film the show here in Canyon Pointe instead of Los Angeles. That way, he's paying less for housing the out-of-town folks. I marked that on page twenty since I'm a local. And . . ." She paused for a dramatic effect.

After several seconds, Harri blurted, "Spit it out, girl!"

Molly clapped her hands. "He wants to film at Lady Jaye's Review! So now, you'll have four clients to juggle!"

CHAPTER 7

Jeremy relaxed against the back of the bench in his booth at La Churro's and sipped his mango margarita. Today's lunch with Elaine went far better than he expected. She already knew all his business procedures. Leonardo would spend the next two weeks walking through beginning and ending of the day routines with her. If she survived the probationary period, the job was hers.

Plus, she had no problem with said probationary period, though she negotiated Jeremy from his desired ninety days to sixty. If everything worked okay with Elaine, Leonardo would start cutting back on his time in the salon, and he'd share Jeremy's chair for those clients they didn't want to or couldn't give up for various reasons. Leonardo could then focus on his design work.

Harri plopped down on the bench across from Jeremy, with her briefcase she used for court. Not a good sign. Without a word, she poured herself a margarita from the pitcher and downed half of it in two gulps before she scowled at him.

"Are you trying to punish me for ignoring your business interests over the past two years?" she said.

"Contract reviews aren't anything new," he protested.

"It is when Molly does a better job of pitching addendums than me." Harri grabbed the pitcher and refilled her glass.

"You sound pissed," Jeremy commented. "Is she insisting on only girl M&Ms in her dressing room for the show?"

"No, the kid should be going to law school, not screwing

around with clothing design." Harri took another gulp of margarita. "Please tell me you ordered queso and extra chips."

The last time Harri plowed through alcohol and junk food like this was after she had fallen in love with Tim Canyon but didn't want to admit it. She was worried about something more than Nix getting into some kind of trouble with the TV people.

"Is representing both me and the kid going to be an issue between us?" Jeremy grinned. "I can always go to Brick Montgomery at Bryson Gaither."

At the mention of the attorney at a rival firm, Harri's hand tightened on her glass. For a split second, it looked like she'd waste good tequila by tossing her drink in his face. Instead, she changed her mind and sipped her drink. At least, she'd stopped gulping it. Jeremy didn't think he could handle a drunk Harri tonight. Neither Dopinder nor any of his cousins would forgive her if she puked in one of their taxis.

"If it comes down to that, you'll all need to get alternate counsel," she said.

"I was joking about the kid." Jeremy reached for the pitcher and topped off his own glass. "Does she really have a problem with me?"

"I don't know if Bernhardt is doing this on purpose, but three of the judges and one of the designer contestants are Winters and Franklin clients."

Jeremy whistled under his breath. Damn, that really put his sisters and Susan in an awkward position. But he knew for Harri, it wasn't about the money. It was about doing the right thing for her clients.

"So what's the plan?" he asked.

"We're going to have a meeting with all the clients involved Friday night." She stopped at the sight of La Churro's owner Mateo delivering their queso and chips. "*Ese*, why are you waiting tables again?"

"I'm only waiting on your table, Winters," the big man said dryly. "And it's only to keep you from poaching any more of my staff."

"Whoa." Harri held up her hands. "Janna's still working here during the evenings."

"But she's not available for the lunch shift thanks to you."

Jeremy wasn't sure if Mateo was really angry or just giving Harri a hard time. But when she glared at Jeremy, he shrugged. "I told him you were joining me when he asked where Leonardo was."

Mateo pulled out an order pad from his apron pocket. "What can I get you two? And by the way, Winters, you'd better give me the same tip you give my staff."

"How long are you going to make me pay for hiring Janna?" Harri asked coolly.

"Until I can find a waitress as good as her or I can train one." Mateo smiled politely at her.

"I'll have the three enchilada plate," Jeremy interjected before Harri did something stupid. Mateo wasn't like his old man back when the girls were in law school. He had no trouble kicking out unruly customers.

"I'll have the beef taco platter. Crunchy, please." Harri handed her menu to Mateo as did Jeremy.

Once the owner strode back to the kitchen area, Harri murmured, "The joke's on him. You're paying tonight."

Jeremy eyed Harri over his margarita glass. "I swear you have a natural talent for creating problems where none exist."

"It's not my fault people make the stupid decisions they do," she grumbled.

"Have you had Timmy and Arthur do a background check on

this Dale Bernhardt?" Jeremy dipped a tortilla chip in the warm queso.

"Arthur's working on it." Harri paid too much attention selecting her own chip. "Did his paramour let something slip with you during their phone call?"

"I only get the impression he's the latest boytoy." Jeremy ate his chip while he reviewed his conversation with Mel this morning. "You think he may have seduced them on purpose?"

"You're going to call me paranoid if I do."

"Shit." Jeremy leaned back against the back of the booth and regarded Harri. "I wish it was just you. But I suppose some idiot had to pick up where Trubble left off."

"I almost wish the genetic testing came back negative." Harri dunked another chip in the gooey cheese.

Jeremy blinked. There was only one reason Harri would be acting this squirrely. "You know, don't you?"

"Know what?" She said around a mouthful of chip and queso.

He pulled out his phone and texted his question.

You know who killed Trubble.

Her phone buzzed. She glanced at the message before she turned her phone face down.

"Yes." She shoved another chip and queso into her mouth.

"And?" He stared at her incredulously.

She slowly chewed and swallowed before she said, "Remember 'Don't ask, don't tell'?"

"If Trubble knew about me, his killer sure as hell does," Jeremy hissed.

"Which was why I was really hoping you and the kids would be going to Los Angeles to record the damn show when I first looked at the paperwork." She sighed and took another sip of her margarita.

"Harri—" He couldn't yell at her like when they were kids.

They were in a public place. Lord only knew how many eyes were on Harri at any given moment.

"Fine," she muttered. "Come back to the Lechuza Building with me after dinner. I'll show you everything."

Jeremy almost said no out of spite, but something said Harri would only make this offer once. Someone considered Byron Trubble, who had been dangerous in his own right, worth kidnapping and killing. If that person wouldn't stop at using a disturbed local attorney to break Trubble out of a supermax prison and shooting the man in the back of the head, they wouldn't hesitate to murder everyone Jeremy cared about.

CHAPTER 8

As much as Harri wanted to order another pitcher of mango margaritas, she didn't. Not with her court-appointed ward at home. She must have looked pretty bad if Jeremy suggested they split a dish of fried ice cream with chocolate syrup.

He avoided sweets, but when he indulged, he preferred honey.

By the time she parked in the Lechuza Building's garage she wanted nothing more than to climb in her bed and sleep the rest of the week away. She hated not being available for her clients, but she never expected Bernhardt to make offers to this many clients at the same time. If it had been only Jeremy and Molly, she'd be able to work things out, but Sabrina Myers was an unknown quantity.

She been recommended by The Yellow Torch, who had been one of Susan's clients before he retired and Susan joined Winters and Franklin. Harri first met with Sabrina during her initial intake interview. She had a clean record, other than a couple of traffic tickets. None of the other attorneys in the firm had any experience with her. And refreshingly, she was a supersuit designer rather than a super.

Jeremy had been Harri's source for assisting Sabrina in building her business. He'd even thrown a couple of new kids her way for designing their supersuits. But if anyone was going to throw a fit, it would be Sabrina.

That wasn't true. Queen Dazzle might throw a fit to rival one of Ultramegaperson's. She would want to be the top judge on the program. And Dazzle would be doubly put out when she found out her ex was Bernhardt's preferred top judge.

Jeremy parked his car and joined her. She punched in her security code. When they entered the foyer, Jeremy looked up and waved.

"Why do you do that? You look like a weirdo," she muttered.

"Because Gracie-poo enjoys seeing her Uncle Jeremy." His grin grew even wider. "And I know it's past her bedtime, so I can't stop in and say hi."

"*Pfft.*" Harri rolled her eyes before she trudged into the Lechuza Building's reception area. She bit her tongue to keep from suggesting he and Leo adopt their own dang kids. Jeremy had never nagged her about the subject of children when she was married to Eddie. Jeremy and Aisha were the only ones who didn't.

The first floor was as quiet as a church until she pressed the elevator button. The antique machinery grumbled to life, and the car itself slowly dropped to the first floor.

Harri opened both gates and stepped into the car. Once Jeremy was inside, she closed the gates. When she pressed the button inside, the car began its slow ascent. Neither of them spoke during the short trip.

And they remained silent after the elevator ground to a halt at the second floor. They exited the car, and Harri stalked down to the spare office she'd appropriated. She unlocked the door, opened it, and flipped on the lights. Steve had helped her nail blankets over the windows so no one could see what was on the walls.

Jeremy stepped inside the office, staring with an alarmed expression as he took in the various pictures, the birth and death certificates, and other paperwork pinned to the drywall. He whistled before he turned to Harri. "Girl, this looks like a stalker's home. Where did all this stuff come from?"

She closed the door and locked it, so none of the kids in the building could "accidentally" come in. "Most of it came from a storage unit Grandma Harri left to me. I didn't have the guts to go check the contents until last summer."

Harri eyed her foster brother. "Jaye, you've got to keep this quiet. You cannot tell Leonardo. There are people willing to kill for this information."

"Kill?"

But she knew which picture had caught his attention. He turned back to Harri, his face a pasty white. She prayed he didn't lose his dinner on her evidence.

"Grandma Harri knew Trubble?" He looked at the photo and back at Harri. "Please, don't tell me she was funding Corvus before she died."

"That's what I feared at first." Harri folded her arms over her chest. "But this information is why Trubble was kidnapped and killed."

"Shit, Harri." Jeremy raked his fingers through his hair, tousling his stylish cut. "What the hell's in here?"

"You remember about four years ago when Seismic Shit allegedly brought down the Lake County Retirement Home by accident?" she said.

Jeremy nodded. "One resident died. And you vowed to make Shift pay for the building after they had to demolish it for being structurally unsound."

"The old man who died was Linwood Baxter, the superhero known as Eagle Forever."

"What?" Jeremy cocked his head. "Are you saying it was a hit?"

"That's what we've spent the last seven months trying to prove."

He turned backed to the picture and tapped the one that had

prompted Susan to put everything together. "Is this the real reason Molly's staying at Aisha's place?"

"Part of it," Harri admitted.

"You really think Rue would pull Kerry and Molly into kidnapping and murder?" Jeremy asked.

"No." Harri walked over to stand beside her brother and stare at the pictures. "But Rue's made a lot of enemies over the years, and the ones still alive are still loyal to Trubble."

"That's why you want me to keep an eye on Nix at the show." Jeremy turned to her. "I know you've told Timmy and Aisha. Who else knows?"

"Only Susan and Arthur." She stared up at him. "I'm serious, Jaye. You can't tell anyone. Not even Leo."

"This needs to go to the FBI."

"We need rock solid proof to take to Consuelo."

"Then the NSB—"

"Wilbur's got one mole left at the NSB he hasn't found." Harri sighed. "And we're certain this one works for Rue."

CHAPTER 9

Harri escorted Jeremy back downstairs and hugged him tightly. Once his car left the garage, she re-engaged the security system. She trudged back to the elevator and went over her to-do list in her head during the slow crawl up to the fifth floor.

Tomorrow, she needed to respond to Mrs. Murphy's claim of keeping Diego from contacting her. Harri needed to draft counter proposals for the Bernhardt Productions offers. Finally, she and Susan needed to consult with Aisha about how to handle Friday's meeting.

Damn, Harri wished Aisha was in the States right now. Her foster sister and best friend was so much better at client care.

She reached the top floor and exited the elevator. A bright purple sticky note hung on her loft door. Ugh. She didn't need to read it to know who it was from.

Harri let herself into her own loft and dropped off her coat and briefcase. A note from Tim on the kitchen island said he and Miguel had taken the boys out for pizza and axe throwing. She squeezed her eyes shut and prayed their ward Diego didn't get hurt. Judge Shriver was going to love hearing about that one after the next home inspection by her court attorney.

Harri grabbed the sticky note. If Molly was having issues with her mother, it was probably a good thing Harri didn't indulge in extra margaritas like she had wanted.

Harri crossed the hallway and knocked on the door. It slid back to show a frazzled Molly. The younger woman wore a Captain Justice t-shirt and denim shorts. Her natural purple and blue hair was clipped into a messy bun.

"Don't ever let Rey or Aisha see that t-shirt," Harri said as she entered the loft.

"Why?" Molly frowned. "Rey's the one who gave it to me."

"Okay, don't let Aisha see it. She's still pissed about throwing all her work on creating Captain Justice out the window thanks to Professor Paranoia." Harri crossed her arms. "What's going on?"

"I want to call Doctor O'Brien. Mom started running a fever around six." Molly shook her head. "The acetaminophen and cold compresses aren't bringing the fever down. Mom said to check with you before I do anything."

That didn't sound good at all. Monica never accepted Harri's advice. "What was the last temperature reading?"

"One-oh-four-point-six about five minutes ago." Molly wrung her hands. "I told her if she hit one-oh-five, I was calling Doctor O'Brien anyway."

Shit. The last thing they needed was the fugitive supervillain dying on them. Harri charged back to the spare bedroom.

"Hey, Short Round." Monica's eyes could barely focus on Harri even with the bedside lamp on. "Tell my daughter I'm fine."

Harri ignored her unwanted guest and laid her palm on Monica's hot, sweaty forehead. Molly wasn't exaggerating. Her mother was burning up.

"Molly, go run a cool bath in the tub."

"Should I put ice in the water?"

"No." Harri pulled her phone out of her pocket and pressed the icon for Hannah O'Brien's cell number.

"What's wrong, Harri?" Hannah blurted.

"I'd like to call you some time when you don't have to ask that question." Harri checked Monica. The fever bright gleam in the supervillain's eyes was not reassuring. "My houseguest is currently running a temperature of a hundred and four. Over-the-counter fever reducers were started three hours ago, but they're not doing a thing. Cold compresses aren't doing a damn thing either."

"Check her wounds," Hannah ordered. "Is there redness, swelling, pus leaking?"

Harri strode over to the bed and flipped up the hem of Monica's damp t-shirt. The supervillain didn't protest, much less move to stop her. "There's swelling and redness around the bandages."

When Harri peeled back the bandages covering the wounds on the woman's abdomen and chest, the supervillain whimpered. "There are scarlet, angry-looking lumps at all three entry points."

The fact that Tim's ex-girlfriend wasn't making any pervy remarks worried Harri even more than the red, swollen lumps.

Hannah swore under her breath. "I'll be over in five minutes. Run a cool bath. We've got to get her temperature down."

"If we can't?" Harri asked.

"We will have to take her to a hospital if we want her to live."

If they took the fugitive Miss Purrception to the hospital, she was dead no matter what the medical staff did. And everyone else involved would be arrested and jailed for aiding and abetting America's most wanted supervillain.

Once again, Harri was thankful she'd offered living space in the Lechuza Building to the firm's four interns as part of their compensation. She had been forced to call Steve for help to get Monica into the tub. Both Harri and Molly worked out on a regular basis, but the supervillain turned into a delirious dead-weight by the time Molly had run the cool bath.

Hannah was as good as her word. Steve's roommate Nick let her into the Lechuza Building and escorted the doctor up to Aisha and Rey's loft. The guys left the bathroom to give Hannah and

Monica a semblance of privacy. The doc set her emergency case next to the tub, knelt on the floor, and started checking vitals while Molly and Harri held their patient's head above the water.

From the agitation in her stomach, Harri feared her perfectly wonderful dinner and margaritas were about to make a reappearance. Molly chewed on her lower lip, probably to keep from screaming. No one needed their eardrums ruptured from the superhero losing control due to her anxiety.

"Doc?" Harri asked.

"I don't know." Hannah shook her head. "How big were those nodules on her abdomen and chest when you called?"

"They're about twice the size now than they were when I changed her bandages around six p.m." Molly said.

As Molly spoke, the largest nodule on Monica's abdomen ruptured, spilling pus and bloody fluid in the bath water.

"Oh, gross!" The superhero leaned away from the tub but still kept a hold on her mom's arm.

A purple capsule bobbed in the disgusting water.

"Wait. What the hell is that?" Harri blinked, but nope, there was definitely something floating in the reddish water.

"Don't touch it," Hannah ordered. She pulled on protective gloves, fished the thing out of the tub, and dumped the capsule into a clear plastic sample cup.

"There's another one," Molly said. A third one bobbed to the surface before Hannah had the chance to retrieve the second.

Once she had the three capsules secured in separate containers, she said, "Would Tim mind if I borrowed his lab when we get Monica stabilized?"

"I don't care if he minds," Harri said. "I'll let you use whatever you want if it keeps her alive and the rest of us out of jail. Steve, I know you're listening. Grab a couple of blankets and all the extra towels from my loft and bring them to the bathroom. Then we'll need your assistance getting Monica out of the tub."

"Is it me, or does Mom feel cooler?" Molly asked.

Hannah stripped off her gloves and held a touch thermometer to Monica's forehead. "One-oh-two-point-one. It may just be the bath though. We'll know for sure when we get her out of the tub, and I deal with those burst cysts."

There was a knock on the bathroom door before Steve said, "I got the towels and blankets, Harri."

"Come in," she called back.

They laid a blanket out on the bathroom floor before Steve carefully lifted an unconscious Monica out of the tub and placed her on it. Harri and Molly dried the supervillain's limbs and hair while Hannah dealt with the open wounds on Monica's chest and abdomen. Steve looked everywhere but at the very naked woman on the floor.

"Bethany's changing the sheets on Monica's bed," he murmured.

"That's good," Harri said. "Thanks for all the extra work you and the other interns are doing. I know it's way outside of your job description."

Steve chuckled. "We're lucky. Most employers say the employees are family, but they don't act like it. You and the partners act like family without saying it. And frankly, Aisha and I wouldn't have gotten Rey back without Monica, so I owe her."

"Hannah, that burst cyst on Monica's chest—" Harri started.

The doctor's expression was grim. "Let's hope the infection isn't in her lungs or heart sac. Let's get her back on the bed, and I'll run an IV with antibiotics."

While Hannah, Steve, and Molly took care of Monica in the bedroom, Harri headed to the kitchen and retrieved rubber gloves and a large garbage bag to clean up the mess in Aisha's bathroom. Nick looked up from the pot of coffee he was preparing.

"You want some help?" he asked.

"No, thanks. I've got it. I need to work off some anger." She nodded at the pot of coffee. "You planning on an all-nighter?"

He shrugged. "Someone's going to need to keep an eye on Molly's mom. We can't afford her dying on us."

Harri swallowed her groan. She was going to get an earful from Tim when he got home. But dammit, it wasn't her fault his supervillain ex-girlfriend kept popping into their lives. And despite Harri's dislike of the woman, she couldn't let her die. She just prayed her staff didn't pay the price for her decisions.

CHAPTER 10

After getting home from dinner with Harri, Jeremy sat in his home office and stared at the profile on his desktop screen. He had to admit Harri's IT guru Arthur Drallhickey was pretty thorough in his research on Dale Bernhardt. There was the usual questionable deals by idiots too enthralled with Hollywood glitter to have their own attorneys look at the contracts, but nothing truly illegal. That was one of the reasons Jeremy appreciated Harri and Aisha's legal skills. His ex-boyfriend forced him to file for bankruptcy because he was too enamored with Ryan's tight ass and talented tongue to see him skimming the till.

The security system beeped to signal someone had come into the loft. Jeremy rose and padded on bare feet out to the living room. Leonardo was hanging up his jacket.

Jeremy walked over and pulled Leonardo into a passionate embrace. When they parted, Leonardo grinned up at him.

"Things went that well during your meeting with Harri?"

"Not exactly." Jeremy took a seat on one of the breakfast bar stools while Leonardo retrieved the take-out containers from the refrigerator. "Bernhardt extended offers to me, Queen Dazzle, and Nix as judges. He also extended an offer to Sabrina Myers to be one of the contestants."

"Ouch." Leonardo popped his entrée into the microwave and pressed the buttons to warm his food. "Is Winters and Franklin going to back out because of the conflict of interest?"

"Harri's scheduled a meeting for Friday night for the partners and clients to discuss the situation." Jeremy pulled the clip off the bag of tortilla chips. "She's not sure how Sabrina is going to handle being judged by the rest of us, and she's worried Queen Dazzle will throw a hissy fit because she's not the top judge."

"This could be your excuse to drop out if you really don't want to do the show." The microwave beeped, and Leonardo pulled out the takeout container and stuck the queso into the microwave. After he started the appliance, he turned to face Jeremy. "You don't want to drop out, do you?"

"I admit my ego's getting in the way." Jeremy shrugged. "But I could pitch Lady Jaye as the hostess and still have a healthy paycheck."

Leonardo frowned and crossed his arms. "So what's really bugging you? The fact that Aisha's not here to review the contracts?"

"That's not fair," Jeremy retorted before he admitted, "Yeah, a little. Harri used to bitch about superheroes with the passion of a supervillain. That's the reason I kept my side hustle a secret from her for so long. Now, she's jumped into the lifestyle with both feet, including marrying a former vigilante super. I don't question her caring about her clients, but with Trubble dead and Aisha in Paris, she's not looking at things with her normal jaded view of the world."

"Honey, why don't you wait and see what happens at this meeting on Friday?" Leonardo carried his dinner and the queso over to the breakfast bar and sat on the stool next to Jeremy. "Get all the information you can before you make a decision."

"You still think I'm going to join Bernhardt's program," Jeremy said.

"If Harri's wants you to keep an eye on Nix, then we both know you'll do it." Leonardo spooned queso over his refried beans and Mexican rice. "She's a sweet kid, but she's terribly naïve.

While Bernhardt wouldn't be stupid enough to cheat on Mel, that doesn't mean one of his co-producers won't take advantage of Nix. You'd be kicking yourself if something did happen to her."

Jeremy dipped a chip in queso and shoved it into his mouth. Leonardo was right. He wouldn't forgive himself if some asshat took advantage of sweet, innocent Nix. The question was whether he could live with himself if he destroyed his and Leonardo's lives in the process.

CHAPTER 11

While Hannah monitored Monica's vitals with the IV running, Harri jogged down the stairs to Susan's apartment. It had taken more than a little convincing for the doctor to let Harri take one of the plastic containers holding an odd purple capsule down to her law partner. Harri had to swear not to open the container. She knocked on Susan's door and prayed the woman wasn't in bed already.

Susan yanked her apartment door open, an alarmed expression on her face. "What's wrong? Please tell me Monica escaped."

"No, but we almost lost her tonight." Harri sucked in a deep breath. "She's fine for now. However, I need to ask a very big favor."

"Come in." Susan chuckled as she stepped back. "I don't have any coffee. Can I interest you in a glass of café zinfandel?"

"How about a half glass?" Harri entered the apartment and shut the door. "I already had enough tequila for dinner."

Susan had her auburn hair pulled up in a messy bun, and she wore a pair of lilac-colored silk pajamas. Her curls bounced as she strode to the kitchen for a glass and the bottle of wine.

Harri secretly wished her own hair had a little *oomph* like Susan's. She hadn't cared enough to even cover her grays when she worked for the city. But to be honest, she hadn't cared about anything back then other than making the heroes and villains pay reparations for the damage they caused during their stupid battles.

Maybe she should let Jeremy do a little more experimenting with her cut and color.

She walked into the center of Susan's living room. A file sat on her coffee table along with Susan's own glass of red wine and a racy romance paperback.

"Please tell me you weren't doing work after hours," Harri said.

"Like you and Aisha don't take your cases up to your lofts with you." Susan grinned as she returned with a half-full glass of red wine for Harri. "My discovery document review is scheduled for tomorrow at the offices of the late, but not lamented, Dewey and Cheatham, provided the trustee doesn't back out. Again." Susan held up her own glass of wine in a bitter salute. "Here's to potentially my last day of ever practicing law again."

"Tim knows what he's doing," Harri said softly as she joined Susan on her overstuffed couch. "I trust him more than I would anyone else to find what we need. He won't get you in trouble."

"I know he wouldn't get busted on purpose." Susan sighed and sipped her wine. "I know I bitched up a storm about illegally searching for the sealed files of the missing super kids, but I hope he can find something that will put Rue Liberty away. Right now, all we have by way of proof is Miss Purrception's word."

"Speaking of Miss Purrception—" Harri pulled the little plastic sample container from her pocket and held it out to Susan. "Don't open it. Hannah's concerned it might be poisonous or carry an infectious agent, but what do you make of this?"

Susan frowned as she held it up to the light. "It almost looks like a super small Magic Grow toy."

"What the hell is a Magic Grow toy?"

"It's a piece of colored foam, usually cut in the shape of an animal. The foam's squeezed down to the size of a medicine capsule and covered with a gelatin. When a kid puts the capsule in water, the gelatin dissolves and the kid magically grows a new toy. Tracy's kids loved this things when they were toddlers." Susan eyed Harri. "Where did Hannah find this?"

"Three of these literally exploded out of Monica's gunshot wounds this evening." Harri explained what happened after she got home from her dinner with Jeremy.

Susan's breath hissed as she held out the container to Harri. "What if there's some kind of tracker in it?"

"I doubt it. The bad guys would have attacked the building when Tim and I brought her here two weeks ago. And that's where the favor I want to ask you comes in." Harri grinned. "I want you to take it to Special Agent Consuelo's office tomorrow."

Susan pursed her lips for a moment before she said, "I thought we'd got beyond me doing firm grunt work."

"If Consuelo and Nesmith want to play games, we can play them, too." Harri shrugged. "Since I'm not supposed to know they've secretly recruited you and Sparx to keep an eye on me, you need to be the person to take it to Consuelo."

"Are you deliberately trying to cause problems between the FBI and NSB?" Susan smirked.

"They're only working with part of the pieces in this particular puzzle," Harri said. "We need to spoon-feed them the rest. I don't want the firm in the middle when Rue Liberty is exposed."

"Sweetie, we're going to be caught in the middle no matter what happens." Susan waved in the general direction of Rue's house. "She's been sucking up to you the last couple of years in hopes of learning whether you had any of your grandmother's evidence of Rue's illegal activities."

Again, Harri shrugged. "I'll cross that bridge when I get to it."

"Has it occurred to you Seismic Shift got the order to kill you from Rue, not Trubble?" Susan took another sip of her wine.

"Yeah, it occurred to me three weeks ago when you pointed

out the evidence had been sitting under my nose for the last several months," Harri said dryly. "Thanks for not rubbing my face in it."

"Tim, Aisha, and I stared at everything you pinned to the walls for the same amount of time as you. It wasn't until Tim and I cleared your spare bedroom for Diego that I notice the connection." Susan set the container on her coffee table. "Where do I tell Consuelo I got our little purple pellet?"

"Tell her as much of the truth as possible," Harri said. "A client of ours was shot trying to stop a murder. Include Monica's symptoms—"

"Without naming her, of course."

Harri took a deep breath to keep her own blood pressure from exploding. "I'm not going to repeat the argument with you about turning her in."

"Girl, this time I agree with you. Miss Purrception is a dead woman if she goes back to Mauvaises. Black Death may be in solitary confinement, but now, we know he doesn't have to touch someone to kill them."

"Thank you," Harri said. "I don't want Steve to do something stupid if you try to turn her in."

"But what are we going to do with her?" Susan asked.

"I don't know. Right now, I'm simply praying she doesn't die tonight." Harri downed her glass in two gulps. "And I'm not the religious type. Thanks for the wine, and thanks for dropping the purple pellet off with Consuelo."

"De nada," Susan replied.

Harri stood and headed for the apartment door. She paused with her hand on the latch and turned to look at Susan. "Thanks for calling me on my bullshit, Susan. And please, keep doing it."

Her partner nodded. "As long as you do the same for me. You're not the only one who gets on her high horse at times."

They both smiled. Harri left Susan's place, closing the door quietly behind her.

After all the tequila and wine tonight, climbing the one flight of stairs to her loft sounded like too much effort. She walked down to the elevator and pressed the button to go up. It was a good thing she and Susan worked out their issues. She honestly didn't know what she would do if she lost the one partner still in the States.

Her next mission would be to convince her husband to collect the bullets from his ex-girlfriend's safehouse.

CHAPTER 12

The next afternoon, Jeremy decided to take the bull by the horns. Mel's boyfriend dangling his club in front of prospective judges and designers left a bad taste in his mouth. Jeremy sat at his desk and called Dale Bernhardt's office in Los Angeles.

The operator claimed he wasn't in yet, though Jeremy made a point of calling after ten a.m. California time. However, she did transfer Jeremy to Bernhardt's assistant.

"Hello, this is Keisha. How can I help you?"

"Well, Keisha, darling, you can start by telling me why your boss is going around claiming he's using my club to film his latest reality show without bothering to talk to me first," Jeremy said using his Lady Jaye voice.

"Ma'am, Mr. Bernhardt has several different projects going on at any given time. Could you be more specific?"

Jeremy had to give the woman credit. She was polite and professional, not the airhead he'd half-expected.

"This is Lady Jaye of Lady Jaye's Revue," he said. "The story on the Canyon Pointe grapevine is he's luring in judges and designers for his new supersuit designing show by claiming the show will be recorded at my club."

"Ma'am, I assure you Mr. Bernhardt is not luring anyone," Keisha said. "He wanted to get half the roster of judges, designers, and supers signed before he approached you about using your facility in order to show he's quite serious. Can I have Mr. Bernhardt call you in five minutes at this number?"

"Five minutes, young lady, or I assure you I will deliver a queen-sized hissy fit."

"Five minutes," Keisha promised him.

Three minutes later, Jeremy's phone rang. He had to give Bernhardt's office credit for keeping a promise. From Jeremy's past associations with the Hollywood crowd, they generally blew him off unless they wanted something. But then, Bernhardt did want something from him.

"Hello, Mr. Harkness, this is Dale Bernhardt. Or should I call you Lady Jaye?" The man was polite, but not overly jovial.

"Mr. Harkness is fine."

"I apologize for not taking your call right away," Bernhardt continued. "Coincidentally, I was speaking with Elaine Trask, the manager of Hair Quotes. She said I would need to run my request to have some of your staff do hair and makeup for *Make Me a Superhero* by you before she could agree to anything."

"You're just digging into all of my businesses, aren't you?" Jeremy drawled.

"I also apologize for you finding out about my interest in your club through the gossip network," Bernhardt said. "With the buzz the show's getting before we even have everything together, the ABS brass wants a bigger venue. We've already made arrangements to film the show at the Jack Canyon Theater."

"Then I apologize for calling your office in a snit based on rumors." Jeremy sighed. "I should know better."

"Actually, I glad you did call," Bernhardt said. "How would you like to host the program as Lady Jaye? That's the real reason I was considering your club as our original venue."

Oh, boy. Jeremy was glad they weren't on a video call. He could feel his face heat from stepping on a landmine.

He cleared his throat. "Exactly what were you thinking, Mr. Bernhardt?"

"I'm going to lay my cards on the table. I'm currently seeing a mutual friend of ours socially." Bernhardt made a disgusted sound. "It's already in the tabloids, but if you need a reference concerning me, ask them. Anyway, they took me to one of your shows when we were in Canyon Pointe last month. I admit I was impressed by your emcee skills."

"Since we're laying our cards on the table, my hosting the show may be a problem." Jeremy hesitated a moment before he took the plunge. "I'm Mel's designer."

The only sound on the line was a whisper of static for a long time. Harri had beat negotiations tactics in Jeremy's head. He knew better than to say anything, but he also didn't want to cause trouble for Mel.

Finally, Bernhardt chuckled. "I'm glad I was in my car and parked for that one. Does that mean you're agreeing to be my top judge?"

"Slow down a bit." Jeremy grinned to himself. "My attorneys are still looking over the offer letter and contracts. And considering both Winters and Franklin are my sisters, they will be going over everything with the proverbial fine-toothed comb."

"I look forward to hearing from them," Bernhardt said. "Was there anything else we needed to address at the moment, Mr. Harkness?"

"Not at the moment, Mr. Bernhardt. Thank you for calling me back." Jeremy ended the call. Harri wasn't going to be happy about him spilling the beans before she was ready. On the other hand, he didn't want Mel's boyfriend to think Jeremy was messing with him either.

He leaned back in his chair. If Leonardo wasn't such a social butterfly, Jeremy would suggest they follow the supervillains' example and buy their own private island. Then he wouldn't get himself in the middle of these messes.

CHAPTER 13

Harri walked back into the Lechuza Building with a bowl of sopa de caracol for Janna and a plantain baleada for herself for lunch.

"Thank you so much!" Janna grinned. "I love real Latin American cuisine instead of the Americanized crap we serve at La Churro's."

"Hey, that Americanized crap fed me all through law school." Harri handed Janna her bag. "Marta slipped some chocolate cinnamon mousse in both our lunches."

"What's wrong with that?" Their new receptionist cocked her head.

"You'll understand when you're over forty, and you have to run an extra mile to work off a spoonful of a decadent dessert," Harri grumbled. "It's bad enough Javier is sneaking junk food to Diego."

"Teenage boys are growing and they need to eat." Janna pulled out her soup and mousse. She looked inside her bag and produced a foil-wrapped package. "How much do you want to bet these are extra tortillas?"

"Marta's worried you're picking up bad gringo habits, like dieting." Harri shook her head.

Janna grinned. "The new chef Kordell said he likes his girls thicc."

"Mr. Lyons is a client."

A shocked expression appeared on Janna's face. "Please tell me you're joking."

Harri groaned. "Please tell me you haven't slept with him."

"We're still at the flirting stage." Janna's lower lip quivered. "Damn."

"Look, honey, I'm not telling you what to do—"

Janna made a face. "Harri, you tell everyone in this building what to do."

"He's a sweet guy under the attitude. Please don't hurt him."

"Yes, ma'am." Janna gestured at her food. "Thanks for buying me lunch."

"De nada." Harri started toward her office, but she paused and turned back to Janna. "Have Susan or Tim called?"

Janna shook her head. "Susan said she expected them to be at Dewey and Cheatham all day. I can't believe the bankruptcy trustee is suing Mother Defiant."

"Keep your fingers crossed Susan and Tim can find what they need to get the asshole off our client's back." Harri stalked into her office and shut the door. It still peeved her the state legislature hadn't passed any anti-SLAPP laws. The bastards at Dewey and Cheatham had nearly bankrupted Mother Defiant between overcharging her for representation and skimming from her income.

Harri sat down at her desk and typed in her password. She nibbled on her lunch while she skimmed through emails until one brought her to a halt. Brick Montgomery, the attorney for Diego's mom, had filed a motion for access to the minor on his client's behalf.

Well, crap. The kid didn't want to talk to his mother. With her constant harassing calls and texts, he'd blocked her. She was now accusing Harri of not letting her talk to her son. Like anyone could control a teenager. Like her own foster father Marvin said, all you can do is try to guide the adolescent into making the best decisions possible.

The kid's dad was a little more reasonable. He didn't bug the kid, and Diego called him every Saturday afternoon like clockwork. But then Lisa Ashcraft wouldn't put up with bullshit from her clients anymore than Harri would.

But still, for someone complaining about not having any money, Mrs. Murphy had no problem spending it. Harri would have to draft the answer to the motion as soon as she was done talking to Aisha.

The next email was from Dale Bernhardt's assistant Keisha about a revised offer. Harri frowned as she opened the attached document. She hadn't even responded to the original offer from yesterday yet.

Oh, crap! The revisions were for Jeremy's role in the TV series, greatly expanding his participation. And the production company had doubled their offer.

Harri finished forwarding the offer to her law partners when the intercom buzzed. She punched the button. "Yes."

"Aisha's on line one, Harri," Janna chirped. Patty must be supplying their new receptionist the same cheerful pills she took.

"Thanks." Harri donned her headset before she tapped the blinking light on her office phone. "Hey, girl! How's the Paris life treating you?"

"We're figuring things out." Aisha chuckled. "About the contracts from Bernhardt Productions—"

"Hold that thought," Harri said. "Have you looked at the revised offer I just forwarded to you?"

"A revised offer? Did you start negotiating without me?" Aisha teased.

"No. And when you read the cover letter, don't you dare

scream and wake up my godson." With Paris being eight hours ahead, Harri knew darn well Mitch was already in bed.

"Holy crap on a cracker." Aisha whistled. "I can understand knowing Jeremy and Lady Jaye being the same person, but how'd they find out Jeremy was Ultramegaperson's supersuit designer?"

"Somebody told them."

"Come on," Aisha protested. "The last thing Ultra would do is out a fellow Alphabet."

Unfortunately, she was right. Harri picked up her pen to jot down names, but only one in particular came to mind, and she thought she'd taught her brother better than to negotiate without an attorney present.

"You got time to chew out our favorite sister for being a stupid butthead," she muttered.

"Always," Aisha said. "I can't believe he'd be that careless. Once someone in La-La-Land knows your secret—"

"It's no longer a secret," Harri finished. "Give me a second to conference him in. This may make our conflict of interest problem a lot easier."

CHAPTER 14

Jeremy doodled with a new idea for Amperage's supersuit on his tablet when his home phone line rang. Since no one outside of immediate family had this particular number, he picked up the receiver. "Hello?"

And immediately wished he hadn't.

"Did you talk to Dale Bernhardt or one of his people without us?" Harri demanded.

"What do you mean?"

"Jaye, be straight with us," Aisha said.

"Is Susan joining you for your little beat on your brother session?" he teased, but the girls weren't in a light-hearted mood.

"Oh, god." Harri groaned. "You did."

"What did you say to who?" Aisha snapped.

"I called Bernhardt because I didn't like him holding my club over people's heads without talking to me first." Jeremy deliberately slurped his ice tea because Harri hated when he did that.

"If you were that pissed about it, why didn't you let me address it with him?" she asked.

"Because I don't need my sisters to fight all of my battles," he shot back. "When I asked Bernhardt about using the club, he said the network expected big things. They're filming the show at the Jack Canyon Theater."

"Dammit, Jeremy!" Aisha muttered. "Has it occurred to you Bernhardt might be lying, and you just threw away a ton of passive income?"

"He wanted Lady Jaye to host the show to begin with," Jeremy said. "I didn't feel right about leading him on, so I told him I was Mel's supersuit designer. I can't do both jobs, but if it means I lost both, then que sera sera."

"Bernhardt does want you to do both jobs," Harri said.

Jeremy straightened in his chair. "He does? Really?"

"The e-mail came in while I was picking up some lunch," Harri said. "Susan's out of the office today, and it's late in France. Can you give us twenty-four hours to review the revised offer with out you doing something stupid?"

"Sure." Jeremy was kind of curious about how Bernhardt planned to handle the dual roles, but now wasn't the time to ask. Not with both Harri and Aisha ready to throttle him for calling Bernhardt on his own.

"We're serious, Jaye," Aisha said sternly. "Keep your damn mouth shut, or find a new firm to represent you. We don't need the shenanigans."

Harri barked at lot, but if Aisha was issuing threats, the girls would definitely toss him out on his ass.

"Cross my heart," he replied.

"Are you going to be okay with the other Winters and Franklin clients knowing about your revised offer?" Harri asked.

"Yes."

"All right," Aisha replied. "I'll get to digging into the fine print. I'll send you my analysis before you go to bed."

"Get some sleep, girl," Harri chuckled.

"I will, but please text me about how things went with Susan this afternoon." Aisha signed off the call.

It didn't mean Jeremy was off the hook with Harri, and he knew it.

"I swear to god, Jaye, if you ever do something like this again—"

"You'll have Steve launch me into orbit because Aisha's on the other side of the planet," he finished.

"I'm glad we understand each other," she muttered.

"Now, are you going to tell me what really crawled up your butt?"

She sighed. "Diego's mom is trying to cause trouble again."

"You know Judge Shriver won't put up with her BS," he assured Harri.

"I can only deal with one crazy person at a time," she warned.

"I'll behave myself, sweetie."

"You'd better."

The line went dead, and Jeremy replaced the receiver in its cradle. Unfortunately, his sisters were right. He did something stupid because he let his ego get in the way. Leonardo would admonish him, too, when he learned about it. Jeremy could already hear his husband's reprimand about acting like a cis-het gorilla.

Maybe the Hollywood glitter blinded him, but in a different way. Regardless, Harri was right. He needed to get his act together.

Especially if he'd be dealing with a supervillain on the set of the show.

CHAPTER 15

It was after six that evening before Tim burst into Harri's office with Susan right behind him. He slapped a handful of files on her desk with a nearly maniacal expression and crowed, "We got 'em!"

"You got them," Susan protested. "I had nothing to do with this."

Harri frowned as she flipped the top file open. "There should be more than this." Her mouth dropped open as she scanned the top couple of sheets. "What the ever loving fuck!"

Tim closed her office door so no one else could hear her tirade, especially the younger residents of the building. Damn, and she'd been doing so good about watching her language since her god-daughter Grace was born.

She looked up at Tim and Susan. "Does Gobert have any idea what's in the Dewey and Cheatham files?"

"No," Susan said bitterly as she flopped on one of Harri's office couches. Harri swiveled her chair to face her law partner as she continued. "On the bright side, my favorite bankruptcy trustee has agreed to sit down with a mediator after his people finally reviewed the discovery they demanded from us."

The court-appointed trustee Peter Gobert may have the stubbornness of a mule, but even he couldn't deny Mother Defiant had crossed her T's and dotted her I's when she fired Dewey and Cheatham as her lawyers and agents.

"However, I think State Senator Wild may be able to use this case to get the anti-SLAPP bill passed," Susan continued.

"You know Gobert's going to want an NDA," Harri said.

"He's not going to get it." Susan smirked. "Mother Defiant was very adamant on that point. I had to point out to Gobert that taking this case to court wouldn't be smart, considering our client's power set."

"Well, her ability to make others tell the truth would prevent any perjury." Harri returned her law partner's grin.

"Tell her what happened when we stopped at the FBI office." Tim crossed the floor and sat on the other couch.

Susan sighed. "Consuelo admitted an agent who was a super, but not part of the underwear brigade, was shot and killed by a similar bullet four weeks ago."

Harri leaned forward on her chair. "Before they found Trubble's body?"

Susan nodded. "He had infiltrated a super supremacist group. The names he was able to pass on were all fake. Phone numbers were for burner phones. All the addresses were cleared out by the time Consuelo could get the search warrants. According to the FBI lab in D.C., there's some kind of macrophage in the pellet that slows down the healing process in a super."

"That explains why Serena couldn't heal Monica's wounds and nearly burned out her own abilities in the process," Harri mused before she returned to her other concern. "Did she press you on where you got the pellet?"

Susan snorted. "Of course, but give me a little credit."

"But she's going to put you guys and Hannah together eventually, Harri," Tim said. "You need to be more careful pulling her into our messes. And I need to change before Steve and I perform our little errand."

Susan groaned. "Do I want to know?"

"We have the location of some of these funky bullets and per-mission from the legal owner to retrieve them." Tim stood.

"Let me guess." Susan rolled her eyes. "My next mission will be to take the bullets Tim and Steve recovered from Miss Purrcep-tion's safehouse to Consuelo and lie my ass off again."

"This is why you need to be more of a loose cannon like my wife," Tim teased. "By the way, I'll make a healthy snack for Di-ego, but Kordell is bringing dinner with him when his shift ends."

"Crap." Harri groaned. "Is he making Emilio clean the grill again?"

"This is Emilio trying to prove to Rueben and Rey he can pull his weight in their little food empire." Tim walked over and kissed her. "We shouldn't be too late, but don't wait up." He strode out of her office, closing the door behind him.

It was so good to see him shed his cane and walk normally again. After Professor Paranoia and his mind control powers forced Steve to attack Tim, the doctors had warned her and Mi-guel they may have to amputate Tim's left leg. Not that his right leg was in much better shape after all the years he spent as a vig-ilante fighting supervillains with actual powers. But the replace-ment knees made a heck of a difference.

"Harri?" Susan watched her with a bit of concern.

"I'm sorry." She tried to shake off her misgivings. "What did you say?"

"What Tim did today at the old Dewey and Cheatham offices was far more risky than what he's doing right now," Susan said. "And he'll have Steve with him this time."

"I can't help worrying when it comes to Monica," Harri ad-mitted.

"He loves you."

"That's the problem." Harri shot Susan a rueful smile. "She

wanted to make it permanent with Tim, and he turned her down. I think her jealousy is why she keeps inserting herself in our lives."

"Thanks, Harri."

She cocked her head. "For what?"

"Trusting me enough to talk about this stuff." Susan shrugged. "I guess I was a little jealous myself. You and Aisha have known each other for a long, long time. I felt like a literal third wheel." She held up her hands. "Which was totally understandable under my temp contract with you. But when you guys offered me the partnership, I assumed things would change."

Harri sat back in her chair and laughed at how Aisha played her. "That's part of the reason Aisha went to Paris now."

Susan open her mouth, but Harri waved her hands.

"I'm sorry," she said in a rush. "I don't mean she's avoiding either of us. It's her way of making me grow up and take responsibility for my relationship with you. I really am sorry I was making you feel like you weren't part of the team. Maybe this weekend we could go to Nolan's for drinks and dinner."

"If you throw in a couple of slices of their peanut butter pie, you're on." Susan grinned. "Let me bring in the boxes from the minivan. I'll need to separate out the files from Tim and the ones for Mother Defiant's case." She hesitated a moment before she said, "Can I ask what he found? He wouldn't show those folders to me. He insisted you needed to see them first."

"You cracked the case. You have the right to have the next look." Harri stood and crossed to the couch. She handed the three files to Susan before she sat next to her law partner.

Susan read through the files, her face, neck, and ears gradually turning the same shade as her hair. "They adopted out non-powered kids to allegedly protect them, then extorted the biological super parents and grandparents?" Her expression when she looked at Harri was one of total fury.

And she was rather glad she wasn't on the receiving end of Susan's rage.

"It explains how Rue Liberty funded her little group." Harri shook her head. "Between her doing this crap and Trubble recruiting actual super kids for his private army, it also explains why Grandma Harri and Eagle Forever started their Underground Railroad for supers."

"If Rue had been extorting Eagle Forever . . ."

Harri nodded. "Either he discovered Rue was behind the extortion, or he knew all along and decided to blow the whistle. I'd like to believe Eagle Forever wasn't stupid enough to have the evidence with him at Lake County Retirement Home, but it's the only explanation for Seismic Shit to kill him. If Eagle Forever had any evidence with him at the retirement home, Seismic Shit took it and murdered Eagle Forever before he brought that section of the building down on the corpse to make it look like an accident."

"And why she sent him after you." Susan whistled. "They wanted any evidence your grandmother had about Rue. I hate to say this—"

"Girl, I've been thinking the same thing for a while." Harri cocked her head. "You think Mother Defiant will agree?"

"As long as you don't mind her knowing about this stuff." Susan handed the folder back to Harri.

"You've got to emphasize to her that if she blabs a word to anyone, she and Blue Racer are dead." Harri smiled. "I heard he finally proposed."

Susan laughed. "Yeah, but she's refusing to set a date until we deal with the breach of contract lawsuit."

"Smart decision," Harri said. "We are a community property state."

"I figured that's why Tim Canyon wanted a sugar momma who wouldn't hide assets from him," Susan teased.

"You know you don't have to unload Aisha's minivan yourself," Harri said. "That's what the interns are for."

"Oh, I plan on using them." Susan handed the folders back to Harri and stood. "And I'm going to hold you to Nolan's on Saturday." She strode out of the office.

Harri stared at the folders in her hands. So much death and destruction. No wonder Seismic Shit was so pissed when she went after him for restitution when she was the Canyon Pointe city attorney. Damn, her days in City Hall felt like a lifetime ago.

If she could supply Consuelo and Wilbur Nesmith, the head of the Canyon Pointe NSB office, enough pieces they could put the puzzle together themselves, it would be safer for her family and friends. She just needed to keep her sanity long enough to finish the job.

Chapter 16

For the first time in a long while, Harri's nerves rang with the intensity of a five-alarm fire. Tim helped her set up the international video call with Aisha on the conference room's huge monitor.

When her partner popped up on the screen, Harri laughed. "It's two-forty-five in the morning in Paris, and you're all decked out." The time difference was why she chose Friday evening in Canyon Pointe. Rey didn't have classes on Saturday, and it would give her best friend a chance to sleep in.

"It's a client meeting, and I dressed appropriately," Aisha shot back.

Harri couldn't argue. The green silk sheath dress and the double string of pearls made Aisha look like the competent, high-powered attorney she was. She even wore makeup, which would be scrubbed off the moment the call ended.

"Where's Susan?" Aisha asked.

"She's at the door, letting the clients in."

Aisha made an unladylike snort. "Arthur could have done that."

"Not tonight," Tim said.

Aisha's eyebrows rose. "Is it what I'm thinking?"

"If I tell you, are you going to wake my godson?" Harri griped.

Her best friend and sister squealed. "Finally! Where's he popping the question?"

"Nolan's."

"Awesome! Did he reserve the back room?"

"I did," Harri snapped. "He was going to take any old table."

Tim leaned close and kissed Harri's cheek. "I'm going to hang out in Arthur's office while you two plan a wedding that's not yours. Talk to you later, Aisha. Give Mitch a hug and kiss from me."

"I will," Aisha promised. They were still discussing Arthur's long-awaited proposal to Patty when Jeremy entered the conference room.

"We've got a second wedding for this year?" He waved at the screen as he passed in front of it. "Hey, sis!" He sat on the first chair to Harri's left. She recognized the power move, but she wasn't going to call him out on it. Not tonight. She needed all the clients in a good mood.

"Possibly," Harri said while Aisha waved back at Jeremy. "That's assuming Arthur doesn't chicken out at the last minute."

"Harri!" Jeremy and Aisha yelled at the same time.

The elevator ground to a stop, and the three of them immediately quieted. Molly bounced into the conference room in her Nix wig and gear.

"Jeremy, I need to make an appointment with you to simplify my look," she blurted as she flopped on the chair to his left. "If I'm going to college this summer, I need to ditch the wig and have an outfit I can get in and out of a lot faster. And if we can all make a deal tonight, we can debut the new look on the show."

"Nix, sweetie, I love you, but could you start with hello?" he said.

"Are we going to be the judges who butt heads throughout the season?" She grinned.

"Um, Harri, why are we even here?" Aisha quipped.

"To eat the snacks?" Harri reached for a chicken taquito.

"I can't eat the snacks through a video call," Aisha complained.

"You're here to make sure our asses are legally covered—" Jeremy said. At his abrupt pause, Harri looked at the doorway.

Sabrina Meyers stood stock still, starstruck as she stared at Molly. The blonde wasn't much older than the superhero, but her face lit up like a Christmas tree. "Ohmigawd! Nix! I'm such a big fan! You're really going to be a judge?"

"Sure am!" Molly grinned beneath her mask.

"Nix, this is Sabrina Meyers," Harri said. "She's also a super-suit designer."

The blonde scurried over to Molly as fast as her black pencil skirt would let her. "I hear you'll be designing your own clothing line for this fall."

The superhero grinned. "With my partners. Don't worry. I'm not trying to intrude on yours or Jeremy's territory. My dresses are more for the average high school girl—"

"Or boy?" Jeremy prodded.

Nix shot him a dirty look before she continued, "—who wants a little more glitter in her life."

Jeremy leaned closer to Harri and whispered, "I don't mind her poaching my clients, but I'd like her to at least acknowledge my presence."

"You know I love you, you silly queen!" Sabrina walked around Nix, Jeremy rose, and the two supersuit designers hugged. "It's just you're my mentor, and she's Nix! I'd be as excited if I met Sparx!"

Harri suppressed the urge to roll her eyes. Sparx wasn't the most sociable person at the best of times. With adults, anyway. Kids were a whole different package, and she'd bend over backward to accommodate her youngest fans. With her own son on the spectrum, Sparx was exceptionally gentle and kind to the children.

Sabrina returned to the other end of the conference table and grabbed a bottle of water before she sat on Nix's left. The two women talked fabrics and the colors for this spring in the fashion industry.

A conversation that would have left Harri in tears if they weren't her clients. She crossed her fingers. If Nix and Sabrina continued to get along this well, maybe tonight's negotiations would be successful.

". . . I want to tone down the glitter that's overwhelmed the young adult styles the past couple of years—"

"Darling, one can never have enough glitter!" Queen Dazzle sashayed into the room. The superhero queen from Queens didn't bother with her public supersuit tonight. She wore a lime green pantsuit with huge white buttons. Her glasses, costume jewelry, purse, and shoes matched her suit's buttons. Her wig was a dark brunette with lime green highlights that matched her suit.

She approached Harri, who rose, and they air-kissed before she turned to Harri's brother. "Letting Jeremy out to play, are we?"

Harri hated being right. Dazzle's attitude may be a major problem tonight.

Jeremy nodded to Queen Dazzle. "I didn't have time wax my legs."

"A queen, super or not, should always make time for grooming," Dazzle responded.

Thankfully, Susan entered the conference room before Harri had to break up a fight and asked if anyone wanted something to drink besides water before they started.

Once everyone was settled with snacks and the beverage of their choice, Harri stood. "Here's the deal, folks. You are all Winters and Franklin clients. You've all received offers from Bernhardt Productions to participate in the reality show *Make Me a Superhero*. Mr. Harkness, Queen Dazzle, and Nix as judges. Ms.

Meyers as a contestant. We've already disclosed to Mr. Bernhardt that Ms. Meyers was once a protégé of Mr. Harkness. He thinks that's great because it will add a level of drama to the competition."

"The second issue is that Mr. Harkness is mine and Ms. Winters' foster brother," Aisha continued. "Nix is currently loftsitting for me and my husband while we are in Paris for the rest of this year. These relationships are potential areas of conflict in addition to you all working for the same production company."

Susan picked up the narrative. "What it comes down to is whether you believe we can and will negotiate for each of you to the best of our ability without shortchanging any of the other three. There's not going to be any secrets. You're each going to know what compensation the other three are getting."

"As I said to each one of you over the phone, this is an all or nothing situation. Either you four agree we can represent you collectively, or we need to refer you each to separate counsel." Harri eyed each client as she spoke.

"Is everything on the table?" Dazzle asked.

Harri nodded.

"Who's the head judge on *Make Me a Superhero*?" Dazzle demanded.

"Jeremy is." Harri stiffened. This was the make or break moment. "And Lady Jaye will be the host of the series."

Dazzle pursed her mouth so tightly Harri half-expected the superhero's fuchsia lipstick to spurt across the room and stain the pristine eggshell wall paint. Instead, she relaxed and nodded and turned to Jeremy. "It makes sense. You are the top supersuit designer in the country, no matter what Renauld Theiss says."

"And I get that as a designer, I'm not making as much as the judges," Sabrina said. "I'm looking long term, getting some publicity for my business and more contracts down the road."

Nix nodded. "Same with me, only in civilian fashion, not su-persuits. I don't want to be like some of my grandmother's friends and have nothing to fall back on when I can't super anymore."

Everyone turned to Queen Dazzle. She smiled. "Honestly, it will be worth the money I make to watch Jeremy go head-to-head with Renauld on stage. I vote for the collective."

Harri breathed a sigh of relief while Susan passed out the ac-knowledgements of joint representation in the matter of *Make Me a Superhero* for their clients to sign.

She should have known something would go wrong this eve-ning before a crazy person started pounding on the bulletproof glass in the front doors.

CHAPTER 17

Jeremy watched Harri, who wore an expression as if she half-expected someone to cause a fuss. He didn't have any doubt she thought it would come from inside the conference room.

Queen Dazzle rose. "You want me and Nix to take care of it for you, Harri?"

Tim poked his head in the conference room doorway. "That's my job, ma'am. Is it okay if I trespass D's mom?"

Harri sighed. "You own half of the building. Do what you see fit."

Tim grinned and gently shut the conference room door.

"You sure you don't want us to escort the bitch off the property?" Nix asked.

"No, thank you," Harri said. "It's not a super matter."

However, both Susan and Aisha looked like the only reason they weren't arguing with Harri was because of the clients in the room.

Jeremy pulled his phone from his pocket and texted Harri.

You'd better tell me after this meeting.

She must have not only silenced her phone, but turned off the vibration alert as well. He could understand not wanting to discuss Diego in front of her clients, but if the kid's bio family were doing stuff, he wanted to make sure she knew he had her back.

Besides, he'd bonded with the kid over the last few weeks. Diego wasn't the only one who had crazy bio parents.

Aisha had already moved on to the joint contract terms. Jeremy forced himself to pay attention. He could play the angry foster uncle later.

Once the counter terms were hammered out and the non-residents left the Lechuza Building, Jeremy rode the elevator with the female residents. Susan got off on the fourth floor, and on the fifth, Molly headed straight for Aisha's place with a weary goodnight. Jeremy followed Harri to hers and Tim's loft, and they walked in to a major teen rant.

"I can't believe she canceled the service for my phone," Diego yelled.

Harri looked at Tim. "Did you get her trespassed?"

"Yes." He sighed and rubbed the back of his neck. "She also tried to get the Ghost Owl arrested when he showed up after hearing the commotion."

Diego paused in his tantrum. "Was the Ghost Owl really here?"

"Yes, but he was there to keep your mother from hurting herself," Tim said.

"Diego, I know it sucks being fourteen and without a phone, but can you chill for tonight, and give Harri and Tim a chance to get you another one?" Jeremy said.

"I-I'm sorry, guys." Diego kicked the toe of his sneakers against the hardwood floorboards. "Owl, Nix, and Shadowstar keep telling me I need to keep my anger under control."

"It's hard at your age," Jeremy replied. "Hormones are seriously messing with your head. But if I can survive Harri going through puberty, you'll manage. Why don't we go get some ice cream while the foster parents talk?"

"I'm not a little kid," Diego muttered.

"Yeah, but I'm the coolest aunt you'll ever have," Jeremy teased.

Diego snickered. "Fine, but you're buying."

"Didn't expect otherwise, my man."

"Where are you two going?" Harri frowned.

"The Arrow Superstore on MLK," Jeremy said. "I won't leave you out. We'll get all the fixings for sundaes and come straight home. I've got my phone, and I promise not to lose your court-appointed ward."

Harri laughed and shook her head. "Don't forget the maraschino cherries."

It was a fairly warm night for winter in Canyon Pointe, so Jeremy put the top down on his sports car before they exited the Lechuza Building's garage.

"I just don't get my mom," Diego said. "She wants me home, but when I was home, she constantly threatened to kick me out. My real dad is more like Tim, you know. He gave me some room after the judge assigned Harri to take care of me. We're talking again. Talking like we used to before I . . . changed."

"Parents tend to look at you one of two ways," Jeremy replied. "You're either the crying baby from the delivery room, or they view you as their clone and place all their unrealized expectations on you. It's hard for them to see you as your own person. If your dad's trying to make that leap, that's a good thing."

"I don't think my mom ever will." Diego stared at the passing buildings as they zipped down Sixth Street.

"I hate to say this, but she may not." Jeremy sighed. "It's been almost thirty years since my parents found out I was gay, and they won't have anything to do with me. I tried a couple of times in my twenties to reconcile, but they wouldn't. It sucks, but on the other hand, my best friends look out for me, then and now. And I got really lucky with Aisha's parents taking me in. Marvin and Betty gave me the love I never got from my biological parents."

"Is it bad that I sometimes wish Harri and Tim were my real parents?"

Jeremy chuckled. "Harri hasn't yelled at you yet, has she?"

"She hasn't raised her voice, but she definitely lets me know if I've screwed up," Diego said. "She has this look that says she knows I can do better and she wants me to do better. Tim gets this disappointed sit-com dad expression."

Jeremy laughed. "That sounds about right. Harri's bio parents weren't the greatest either."

"Yeah, she told me about them and her stepmom."

"And that's why she's trying so hard to be careful with you." Jeremy flipped the turn signal for the entrance to the Arrow parking lot.

"Except sometimes, she gets this scared look," Diego added. "I worry she regrets taking me in."

Jeremy pulled into a parking space, shut off the engine, and turned to the kid. "You wanna know the truth?"

Diego nodded.

"She's worried she's putting you in danger by taking you in," Jeremy said. "Javi's baby brother was kidnapped by someone trying to kill Harri. Patty's ex boyfriend tried to kill people at our sister Aisha's wedding because Harri made sure he didn't get custody of her goddaughter. Another nutcase tried to shoot up hers and Tim's wedding on New Year's Eve. That's why she gets the worried expression. She and Tim don't regret for one second about accepting you in their home."

"Okay." Diego nodded. He even looked a little relieved beneath the parking lot's security lights.

"Now let's get that ice cream." Jeremy winked.

As they walked toward the store's main entrance, Jeremy prayed he'd said the right things to the kid. If Diego ran away . . .

Well, the street was no place for any fourteen-year-old, even if he did have superpowers.

CHAPTER 18

A week later, an intern for the production company led Jeremy to the back room of the Jack Canyon Theater for the judges' meeting. Dale Bernhardt and his assistants had flown into Canyon Pointe to meet with them and go over his expectations during the filming next month.

After a long talk with Susan and his sisters, Jeremy decided to come out of the closet, so to speak. He'd dressed some of the most well-known superheroes in the country. Plus, Timmy had created custom software with an encrypted database years ago so Jeremy could protect his clients' identities.

When he entered the room, Dale's face lit up and he stood. "Jeremy! Nice to meet you in person!" He held out his hand, which Jeremy shook. "Everyone, this is Jeremy Harkness, our chief judge."

There were four people in jeans and t-shirts, besides the girl who had escorted him to meeting, who he didn't know. Nix and Queen Dazzle wore their superhero garb. But Renauld Theiss and Isabella Wang were dressed to the nines.

Wang eyed him as if he were a potential competitor. Theiss, however, jumped to his feet.

"You said Mr. X would be the chief judge!" Theiss waved his arms wildly. "I am not going to share the stage with some unknown hack!"

"Sit down, Renauld!" Queen Dazzle snapped. "Jeremy Harkness is Mr. X. Both I and Ultramegaperson verified his identity to Mr. Bernhardt. Assholes like you are the reason Jeremy maintained his secrecy for so long. And you even admitted to me, Captain Justice's outfit was the most incredible supersuit you'd ever seen, and you wished you'd been the one to create it!"

Theiss's mouth fell open, and he stared at Queen Dazzle for a long time before he said, "Are you firing me?" His French accent grew thicker with emotion.

"No, darling." Queen Dazzle gave an exaggerated sigh. "Jeremy may be my ex, but we separated on good terms, so I'm not going to tolerate you starting something here."

The designer lowered his arms. "My apologies, Mr. Harkness. And to you, Mr. Bernhardt."

"A pleasure to meet you, Mr. Harkness." Isabella Wang nodded.

"The pleasure's mine." Jeremy smiled politely at the woman. "I've admired your work for some time."

Both he and Bernhardt took their seats. The intern handed Jeremy a printed package, laying out the show's concept, and Bernhardt launched into his plans, which included keeping Jeremy's identity secret until the very last episode.

"We'll have you wearing a plain black cowl and bodysuit in the first episode," Bernhardt said. "However, I'd like to see you wearing some replicas of your clients' outfits between the first and last episodes.

"That's fine for the judging portions of the show." Jeremy tapped his stylus against his personal tablet he was using for notes. "But what happens when both Mr. X and Lady Jaye are supposed to be on stage at the same time?"

Burnhardt turned to one of the assistants. "Jeff?"

The kid stood. Jeremy estimated he was about five-ten, maybe a hundred-sixty pounds at most. His dark hair, dark eyes, and medium skin tone would make him stand out in a Midwestern crowd.

Except Jeff's hair seemed to be getting lighter. Jeremy blinked. The kid grew taller and a little broader in the shoulders, stretching his Taylor Swift concert t-shirt until it was skintight. His features shifted, and his irises lightened from dark brown to gray-blue.

Jeremy found himself, looking at his double. "Wow! And why hasn't the NSB snatched you up?"

"Because I'm registered, Mr. Harkness." Jeff's voice was a perfect imitation of Jeremy's. The kid shrugged. "I'm still putting together everything to go public as a suit. I can't afford a designer like you, Mr. Theiss, and Ms. Wang, so I'm hoping to check out the work of the contestants."

"And hire them cheap." Theiss sneered.

Jeff lifted his chin. "You three were all beginners at one time."

"The more important thing is making sure you've got an established super to train with," Jeremy said. "You got someone?"

The kid nodded. "Please don't ask me who it is."

"Wouldn't dream of it," Jeremy assured. "But could you stop looking like me for a now? It really creeps me out."

Jeff grinned. "No problem." He shrank down, his coloring darkened once again, and sat in his chair.

"Mr. Bernhardt?" Wang said. "I do have concerns about having a supervillain around so many civilians. While I have no doubt, Queen Dazzle and Nix would do their best to protect us, I fear someone, especially a contestant, might get hurt."

"I'd be more worried about one of up-and-coming supers getting themselves hurt or killed," Nix spoke for the first time. "It's never as easy as it looks."

"First of all, the audience members will have to sign waivers that they understand the potential danger of being voluntarily in the presence of a supervillain," Bernhardt said.

Jeremy made a note on his tablet of asking Harri about liability. He doubted such a waiver would hold up in court.

"Second, the super who claims to be a supervillain has not committed any crimes." Bernhardt chuckled. "Yet. However, they have been warned, verbally and in writing, the commission of any crimes during the filming of the series or the airing of the series will result in the forfeiture of their awards for being a part of *Make Me a Superhero*, and everyone on the production will cooperate in filing charges with the FBI."

Jeremy wondered if the kid playing the supervillain on this show was more like Harri's IT guy. Arthur Drallhickey, AKA Professor Venom was a nice guy who had been screwed by the system and his own parents. His anger went to the wrong place. Back when she had been the Canyon Pointe city attorney, Harri realized Arthur was more of a danger to himself than anyone else.

"As for the super contestants, they are not licensed for heroics yet," Bernhardt continued. "In fact, a publicity package and assistance with getting licensed is the super winner's award. Again, they've all signed the notice that any heroics performed during the course of the filming or before the show's finished airing on ABS will result in forfeiture of their prizes."

Isabella smiled. "So, what happens if your alleged supervillain wins the supers' portion of the contest?"

"We will do our best to steer them towards a different path," Bernhardt said calmly.

Jeremy glanced at Nix. She didn't look too happy, and he couldn't blame her. The network and production company were essentially funding someone who planned to commit crimes. He jotted down another note to ask Harri whether this was supporting supervilliany. He'd hung around his sisters too long not to be aware of his potential liabilities.

"I hope you know what you're doing," Queen Dazzle murmured. "If this supervillain wannabe goes really bad, this will af-fect mine and Nix's reputations and therefore, our bottom lines beyond what you're paying us."

"The production company has more than sufficient insurance to cover any damages that might occur." Bernhardt didn't seem to be taking Queen Dazzle's comments personally.

Jeremy needed to find the insured amount for *Make Me a Su-perhero*. He didn't want to end up dead if some executive decided he'd rather collect an insurance check rather than make sure his employees were safe.

CHAPTER 19

The following Monday, Harri drove to the Family Court Building with Diego in her passenger seat. Despite the court representative doing a home inspection, despite the police record of his mom being trespassed from the Lechuza Building for harassment, despite a statement from the Ghost Owl corroborating the police's account of the incident, Brick Montgomery insisted on a hearing on his client's motion.

It didn't help Harri's mood that Diego shivered even though it was already seventy-five degrees this early in the morning.

"Do I have to talk to her?" His voice shook as bad as his body.

"Nope," Harri said. "I'm taking you in the back way to Judge Shriver's chambers. You're going to have your own private conversation with her."

"What do I tell her?"

Harri glanced at her ward, wishing she could do more to console him. "You can tell her whatever you want. All I ask is that you tell her the truth."

"I want to stay with you and Tim," he protested.

"Then tell her that and tell her why you feel the way you do," Harri said. "You've met her before. She isn't a monster. She understands the situation and will do what she has to in order for you to be safe."

"Will that guy from the Superhero Bureau be there?"

She glanced at Diego. At least, he wasn't shaking like he had been a moment ago.

"I don't know." She flipped her signal to turn into the local courts' parking garage. "Unless one of your parent's attorneys or the judge called the NSB, I doubt if an agent will be there."

"I can see Mom doing it to punish me," Diego grumbled. "Like turning off my phone."

Harri clenched her teeth to keep from saying anything bad about Isla Murphy as she guided her ancient sedan up the garage's ramps and searched for a parking place. Because if Wilbur Nesmith was at the court today, Isla's attorney Brick Montgomery called him.

It might be worth going to jail to use the taser embedded in her watch on Montgomery.

Harri left Diego with Judge Shriver in her chambers, and the court clerk Cathy Blanchett guided Harri out to the courtroom proper. Only Diego's father Carl Murphy and Carl's attorney Lisa Ashcraft were present besides the bailiff. They approached Harri in the middle of the well.

"I just want to say thank you for taking care of Diego, Ms. Winters," Carl said. "And especially for replacing his phone."

She cocked her head. "I thought you were paying for Diego's phone service, not Isla."

"We have a family plan under my name." He crossed his arms and stared at the floor. "Part of the settlement was I would continue to pay the service fee for all three phones until our divorce was final."

Harri made a disgusted sound in the back of her throat. "And because it's a community property state, she called your provider and discontinued Diego's service. I had a feeling that's how things went down."

"Any hint on how the judge is feeling about this—" Lisa took a deep breath to keep saying something she shouldn't because Cathy and the bailiff were obviously paying attention to their conversation. "—motion?"

Harri shook her head. "I told Diego to be truthful with her. A lot of it's going to be how she reacts to what he says."

"He doesn't want to live with either of us, does he?" Carl asked mournfully.

"Don't put words in his mouth," Harri said a little more sharply then she intended.

Carl took a half-step back.

She took her own deep breath to calm down. "That's part of the problem. Neither you nor Isla have been listening to him."

"I've been going to a therapist," Carl murmured. "And I've only called Diego once because he didn't call during his normal time on Saturday."

"And you're doing a much better with Diego the last couple of weeks because of your therapy and actions," Harri said. "Both my husband and I have noticed. Don't go back to the old ways now."

Carl nodded.

Brick Montgomery and Isla Murphy burst into the courtroom. She opened her mouth the moment she spotted Harri, but Brick grabbed Isla's arm just below the short sleeve of her flower-patterned dress. And he squeezed hard from her red skin around his fingertips.

He guided her to the right counsel's table and whispered something in her ear. She sat with an ugly, sullen look on her face.

Brick approached the trio in the well with a stiff smile. "May the attorneys speak alone, Mr. Murphy?"

Diego's dad glanced at Lisa, who nodded.

To his credit, Carl said, "I need to get a drink of water. I'll be back in two minutes." He walked out of the courtroom.

When Isla started to stand, Brick barked, "Take your seat, Mrs. Murphy."

She dropped to her chair with a surprised look, but she remained silent.

He turned back to Lisa and Harri. "What's it going to take for my client to see her son?"

Harri lowered her voice. "Brick, she's been calling and texting Diego incessantly since the judge assigned me as his guardian. And by incessantly, I mean twenty-four hours a day. Isla needs to lay off."

"You have proof of this?"

"Yes, the data, call records, and text records from his old phone were downloaded to his new one after she cancelled his service late Friday evening despite Mr. Murphy's agreement to continue paying for the entire family's phone services until the divorce is final." Harri shrugged. "My tech people also made copies of everything. Judge Shriver wanted to speak to Diego first, so she probably knows everything by now."

"Has she been attending therapy?" Lisa asked.

"That's not really your concern," he hissed.

"It is mine," Harri snapped. "My husband is one thing, but when the Ghost Owl says the woman doesn't seem stable as an independent observer, then I listen."

"Th-the Ghost Owl?" Brick's skin grew pasty beneath his fake tan.

"Your client was screaming loud enough Friday night for someone with superhearing to notice." She shook head. "I also got several noise complaints from residents of the Lechuza Building and our neighbors. Though most of them were happy to learn Isla wasn't a supervillain."

Carl re-entered the courtroom. Apparently, that's what the court staff was waiting for.

"All rise," the bailiff called out. Everyone scurried for their places. Harri stepped up to the jury box. When the bailiff finished his announcement, Judge Shriver stormed into her courtroom, looking steamed.

In fact, Harri was surprised the judge's reading glasses weren't covered in mist. She sat in her chair and glared at Isla Murphy.

"Mrs. Murphy, do you realize it's against the law to stalk someone in the State of Mojave?"

Yep, Diego showed the judge the texts sent and messages his mother left on his phone.

Brick stood and nudged his client to do so as well.

"I just want to talk to my son," Isla wailed.

"I asked you a yes or no question," the judge said. A lot more patiently than Harri would have.

"I wasn't stalking him." Isla jabbed her index finger in Harri's direction. "She lets my son talk to his father, but not me!"

Judge Shriver took off her reading glasses and glared at Isla. "Ms. Winters, take the witness stand."

Harri jumped up and strode over to the little square with a chair. She remained standing until the bailiff finished swearing her in before she sat.

"Speak your name for the court record," the judge commanded.

"Harriet M. Winters."

"And I assigned you as the attorney ad litem for the minor Diego Murphy?"

"Yes, your honor."

"And at the request of Mr. Murphy and his attorney, did I name you guardian ad litem for the minor Diego Murphy?"

"Yes, your honor," Harri repeated.

"Did you know about Mrs. Murphy's repeated calls and texts to Diego?"

"Yes, your honor."

"What did you do to stop it?" Judge Shriver still didn't look at Harri. And Isla Murphy was quickly losing her cockiness.

"I told Diego to leave his phone off at night, so he could sleep," Harri said. "When they continued through school hours, I told him to leave the sound off, so his teachers wouldn't confiscate his phone. Eventually, the calling and texting became so bad, Diego asked me if he should block his mother. I told him he should do what he's comfortable with."

"At any time, did you or your husband tell Diego he should not speak with his mother?" the judge continued.

"No, your honor."

"Did you ever take away Diego's phone from him?"

"No, your honor." Harri spoke fast to get the next item on the record. "To my knowledge before today, Diego's parents paid for his phone and plan. He wasn't misusing the device, so there was no reason for me or my husband to take it from him. Our only rules regarding its use were not to use it in class without a teacher's permission and not to use it during our dinner time."

"At any time, did you give any instructions to Diego about calling his father?" Justice Shriver still glared at Isla Murphy, who was sinking lower in her chair.

"No, your honor."

The judge took a deep breath and released it. "Does either counsel wish to cross-examine the court-appointed ad litem?"

Lisa stood. "No questions, your honor."

Isla whispered furiously at Brick. When he answered, he didn't bother lowering his voice.

"You were damn lucky Canyon only had you trespassed, and you're going to be damn lucky if the judge doesn't refer you to the D.A. for charges." He stood. "No questions for the ad litem, your honor."

Judge Shriver finally looked at Harri and smiled. "Thank you, Ms. Winters."

Harri stepped down from the witness stand and crossed the well back to the jury box.

"Mr. Montgomery, you may proceed," Judge Shriver said.

He also took a deep breath to calm himself. "Your honor, at this time, the petitioner wishes to withdraw the motion."

Isla jumped to her feet. "I-I object!"

"Think very carefully about your next words before I hold you in contempt, Mrs. Murphy." The judge's glare was back.

"Sit down, Isla," Brick snapped.

Her mouth opened and closed a few times before she dropped to her chair.

Judge Shriver turned to her court clerk. "Cathy, isn't the hearing on Diego's custody scheduled for the beginning of March?"

"March 6th, your honor."

"Cancel that hearing," the judge ordered. "Move the hearing out to June. Ninety days from the original hearing date. He's making excellent progress at the new middle school. I don't want to disrupt his life before the end of the school year."

Cathy typed the appropriate commands for the court's scheduling software. "That would be Sunday, June 4th."

The judge flipped through the paper calendar on her desk. "The following Tuesday then. The 6th."

Cathy looked up at Harri. "Is one p.m. acceptable, Ms. Winters?"

"Perfect." Harri entered the hearing on her phone's calendar.

"Court is dismissed." Judge Shriver didn't bother to ask the parents' attorneys if the time and date were acceptable to them. She banged her gavel and stalked out of the courtroom before everyone stood.

"She can't do that!" Isla Murphy shrieked.

The bailiff approached the petitioner's table. "Ms. Murphy, I suggest you take your complaints out of the courthouse. The judge wasn't joking about throwing you in jail for contempt."

"Come on, Isla." Brick grabbed her arm and dragged her out of the courtroom. She complained bitterly the whole way.

Lisa rolled her eyes as she grabbed her bag. "Sorry your time was wasted, Harri."

"Um, can-can I talk to my son before we leave?" Carl said. "If it's all right with you, Ms. Winters?"

"It's actually up to Diego." Harri smiled. "But I'll go ask."

She walked back to the judge's chambers and knocked before she pushed the half open door.

"Is she gone?" Judge Shriver and Diego said at the same time.

"Yes," Harri said. "Diego, your dad asked if it would be okay to see you for a few minutes."

"Do I have to?" Except this was a child's timidity, not an adolescent's bluster.

"Only if you want to," Harri said. "The judge and I aren't going to make you."

Diego released a deep breath. "Yeah, I'd like to see him."

"Not alone, Ms. Winters," the judge warned. "I'm not taking any chances with Diego's welfare."

"Understood, your honor." Harri nodded. And she couldn't help noticing Diego's eager stride as she followed him into the courtroom.

Maybe things would work out for the kid after all.

CHAPTER 20

The first day of spring dawned bright and clear when Lady Jaye arrived at the Jack Canyon Theater. She wore her favorite summer frock, a frilly turquoise number with matching jewelry and shoes. Nerves ran through her despite the confidence this outfit normally gave her.

Stage work was one thing. A performer fed off the energy of a live crowd. But today's taping didn't have an audience. Today, the crew was filming the background interviews, bits of which would be interspersed throughout the thirteen-episode series.

But the tickets for the later episodes' audiences had already been given away. The preshow publicity was already in motion. Guards kept the two dozen potential fans from blocking the back entrance, and vans from Action 12! and a few other television stations were setting up. It wasn't everyday a production company came to Canyon Pointe.

Taking a deep breath, she slung her tote bag over her shoulder and strode toward the backstage door. Some of the fans recognized Jaye despite her red wig and started screaming. She waved at them, but five of the guards kept them back. The sixth guard approached her.

He was a lighter skinned Black man. Handsome but for the darker circles beneath his eyes. His name tag read "Murphy".

"Ms. Jaye? I have your passes for the production." He smiled and handed a small manila envelope to her.

She returned, "It's just Jaye, baby doll. Do you mind if I call you Murph?"

"Ma'am, you can call me anything you want."

"But just call you?" Jaye teased.

His smile widened to a full-on grin. It must have been a while since anyone flirted with him. He opened the door for her and lowered his voice. "Just follow the sounds of the screaming little French guy to find the rest of the cast."

Jaye laughed and entered. Neon poster board with writing in crisp black Sharpie lines pointed the way to the makeup area.

In the makeshift salon, three of her employees from Hair Quotes and one of Bernhardt's people worked on cast members while a couple of other kids waited their turn. A chorus of "Hi Jaye"s acknowledged her presence.

Bernhardt's person excused herself from the cast member she worked on and approached Jaye. "Hi, Lady Jaye. I'm Sheila Dorsey, *Make Me a Superhero*'s lead makeup artist." She held out her hand, which Jaye shook.

"Call me Jaye." She released Sheila's hand while the artist examined her with a critical eye.

"I don't think you'll need any touchups, Jaye."

"Of course, she doesn't," Roxanne proclaimed. "She's the one who taught us."

"Jaye's the best with the brush," Phyllis added.

"And she knows color like no one else," Mary concluded.

Sheila grinned. "Jaye, why don't you go to the baby stage? Our assistant director Connie Bancroft will take you from there. By the way, I love the outfit."

"Thanks, girlfriend." Jaye headed back to the hallway and followed the signs to what everyone called the baby stage. It was a smaller theater in the building, designed for a more intimate setting between performer and audience member. It made sense why the director for the series wanted to use it for the individual interviews.

A serious-looking woman in big, black, cat eye glasses, jeans, and an oversized lime green button-down shirt waited outside the stage door. She appeared intent on what someone was saying on her headset.

A half dozen hard plastic chairs lined the hall across from the door. An unknown boy sat in one of them, and Queen Dazzle perched on another with a sly smile on her face and wearing her supersuit. One didn't need superhearing to understand the swearing in French from Theiss through the thick stage door.

"Lady Jaye, I'm Connie, the assistant director." The girl with the clipboard retained her serious demeanor. "Have a seat, and you'll be right after Queen Dazzle."

"Thank you, hun." She perched on the chair next to the superhero and whispered, "I take it Renauld's not happy."

"How could you tell?" Queen Dazzle's words dripped with sarcasm. "He's argued with everyone from the makeup girls to poor Connie. Nor has he been polite to the up-and-coming kids." She inclined her head slightly to indicate the boy sitting on her other side. "He's going out of his way to make them miserable enough to quit."

"It's all part of the game," the kid said with a surety that belied his age. "The other reality shows' play head games to spike the drama and attract viewers." He shrugged. "This isn't going to be any different if y'all are already playing nice judge/nasty judge."

Jaye leaned over to examine him more closely. He had heavy lids and dark, purposely shaggy, black hair with raspberry highlights. His white knit turtle-neck was decorated with a silver zipper across his chest. His look was completed with baggy black twill pants and brilliant red sneakers.

"You're one of the designers, right?" Jaye said.

He nodded and smiled shyly. "Vinh Dang. I'm a big fan. Um, could I get your autograph later?"

"Of course," Jaye said politely. "But you're a little young to be coming to the Revue, aren't you?"

He straightened in his seat. "I'm twenty. My roommate at CU Boulder is from Canyon Pointe. She took me to the Revue over winter break."

"I take it you're majoring in fashion design?" Jaye asked.

Vinh nodded and smiled wryly. "I wish they had a class specifically for supersuits. There's a huge difference between working with Kevlar and working with crepe."

"True." Jaye laughed. "But supersuits and drag are very similar. I can't give you any pointers during the taping of the show, but I can introduce you to some other designers after the show airs."

"That would be great!" Vinh beamed. "Thanks, Jaye."

Queen Dazzle chuckled. "Jaye, you can't adopt all the children participating in this show. You and your darling spouse don't have enough room."

"I'm not adopting anyone," Jaye said archly. "I'm paying it forward. Some of the OG queens in Canyon Pointe took me under their wings when I was Vinh's age. Without them, I wouldn't be where I am today."

"Touché." Dazzle inclined her head.

Vinh snickered. "How long were you two dating?"

Jaye's face warmed at the boy's observation, and Connie's attention perked. Of course, that tidbit would be used for some drama in the program.

"Long enough to know we were better off as friends," Jaye said.

The stage door burst open, and Renauld strode out with an unexpected grin on his face. "I may detest the United States, but this program is going to be delightful trash." The designer practically danced down the hall.

"You're up, Vinh," Connie announced.

Once the kid was safely ensconced in the baby theater, Queen Dazzle turned to Jaye. "I hope that asshat doesn't go too far. Not all of the contestants I've met are as strong or understand the game dynamics like Vinh."

"He's your designer," Jaye said. "Maybe you should talk to him."

"No," Connie blurted. "Please don't. We want to keep the judges acting like their normal selves."

"At the risk of some of the participants' mental health?" Jaye prodded.

"We've got a therapist on staff for both the supers and the designers while we film." Connie shrugged. "Judges, too, if you need to talk to someone. However, the world isn't fair, and if these kids want to make it, they need to understand not everyone is going to like them."

"Kids like Vinh already know life isn't fair," Jaye snapped, her carefully cultivated alto disappearing in her anger. "I don't want the situation to be made worse."

"Your concern will be relayed to Mr. Julien and the producers," Connie said coolly.

Jaye didn't like the assistant director's response, but she let it go for now. It seemed like Nix wasn't the only kid she needed to look out for during the show's production if the people in charge didn't give a shit about them.

CHAPTER 21

On Monday morning, the heady odor of coffee greeted Harri when she carried her laptop and case files over to Aisha's loft. She may be a morning person, but this before dawn crap was for the birds.

"Thanks for watching Mom, Harri!" Molly was already in her superhero togs and wig. She swung on a matching leather jacket. "I really appreciate this."

"So we're back to calling her Mom?" Harri teased.

The parts of Molly's face not covered by her Nix mask turned bright pink. "Almost losing her made me realize how stupid I was acting."

"Believe it or not, I understand how you feel." Harri's dad had done his share of disappointing her when she was growing up. She set her computer and files on Aisha's breakfast bar because she didn't want to disturb Molly's fashion design project spread out on Aisha's dining table. "I can handle babysitting for a few weeks while you film the show." She frowned. "Have you told Monica what you're doing?"

"Yeah, I did." The corner of Molly's mouth quirked. "Would you believe she promised not to leave until I finished filming?"

No, Harri didn't believe Monica would stay put, but she couldn't hurt Molly by saying that. Instead, she said, "Don't take it as an insult. That's the closest she can come to saying she's proud of you."

Molly shook her head. "I don't think Grandma said that

enough to Mom while she was growing up, but I'll take what I can get."

"Have you talked to Rue lately?" Harri hated using Molly to keep tabs on Rue Liberty, but she didn't trust herself to call the old woman without revealing she knew Rue killed Trubble.

"I called a couple of weeks ago to tell her I got the job on *Make Me a Superhero.*" Molly sighed. "Instead of congratulating me, she offered to pay for my school if I moved back in with her."

"What did you tell her?" Harri asked.

"Thanks, but no thanks." Molly sighed again. "It's not that I don't care about her, but I'm twenty-six. I need to grow up and be responsible."

"Speaking of responsible, you'd better get going, kiddo." Harri grinned. "You don't want to be late on your first day."

"Thanks again, Harri." Molly strode over and gave her a bear hug before the kid grabbed her motorcycle helmet and left the loft, locking the door behind her.

While Harri poured herself a cup of coffee, slow shuffling came from the other side of the loft. She forgot to grab her cinnamon creamer, so she checked the fridge. Molly's chocolate caramel crap would have to do for this morning. It still beat Aisha's pixie barf. While she poured a dollop in her coffee, the pipes hummed from water flowing through them. At least, her charge didn't need help in the bathroom. She turned to put the creamer back in the fridge, and the shuffling grew louder.

"Stealing my daughter's creamer?"

Harri closed the fridge door to find Monica smirking at her. At least, the supervillain was clean, upright, and had some color in her face this time. She wore a Sparx bathrobe over Nix pajamas with fluffy Jackalope Girl slippers.

"Did you rob a Hero's World store?" Harri asked.

Monica's smirk disappeared. "No. It's merchandise Molly swapped with other supers."

"Glad to see you're looking a lot better." Harri sipped her coffee. Yep, Molly's creamer was definitely too sweet. Maybe she could beg Susan to bring up some cinnamon syrup from the firm's break room later.

"You mean you're glad I didn't die in your best friend's loft in the building you and my ex own," Monica shot back. She shuffled to the pantry and retrieved a bag of bagels.

Harri decided to ignore the supervillain's bitchy attitude. "I can make an omelet for you."

"I don't need your charity, Winters!" But Monica's outburst obviously overloaded her still healing body. Her knees buckled, and she slumped to the floor.

Harri set her cup on the counter before she stepped to the stubborn supervillian's side and heaved Monica to her feet.

"Timmy making you work out, Short Round?" She sneered.

Harri laugh as she practically dragged Monica to the couch and dropped her on it. "I'm not the one who got shot up by her own mother."

Monica winced as she pushed herself into a sitting position.

"When was the last time the packing on the ruptured cysts was changed?" Harri asked.

Monica grunted as she pulled the crocheted afghan Aunt Queenie had made for Aisha years ago from the back of the couch and around her shoulders. "O'Brien removed the packing last Friday, and Molly changed the bandages this morning."

"Improvement is good," Harri said. "You rest. I'll make breakfast. You want coffee or juice?"

"Can I have both?" Monica said a little more politely than before. "Molly has some grapefruit juice in the fridge for me."

Harri dragged over the ottoman so Monica could prop up her feet and set up a TV tray for her. After Harri delivered the requested black coffee and grapefruit juice, Monica flipped the channels and settled on Action 12!'s morning show while Harri mixed up a cheese omelet and toasted a plain bagel.

On Rey's giant screen, Misha Winchester and her co-host Stone Westinghouse prattled on about last night's awards show and who wore what.

"Hollywood's latest It couple, superhero Ultramegaperson and producer Dale Bernhardt, graced the red carpet in a matching dress and suit by Isabella Wang," Misha announced.

Harri looked up from the skillet. Ultra wore a white sleeveless mermaid dress covered in tiny crystals. The color set off their dark skin and rainbow-colored hair. Instead of their usual mask, Ultra used white glittery makeup with crystals glued to their skin in a mask shape around their eyes. Bernhardt's black suit had strategically placed crystals along the outside seams of his trousers and the jacket's lapels and collar. The couple looked incredibly happy.

Harri placed the finished omelet on a plate and smeared cream cheese on the toasted bagel. When she carried the plate, napkin and silverware to Monica and sat them on the TV tray, the supervillain looked up at her.

"Do you think Ultramegaperson is really happy with that guy?" Monica asked.

"I don't know." Harri examined the supervillain's face. She seemed . . . sad. "Why do you ask?"

"I'm wondering why the women in my family keep picking the wrong guys."

"Kerry's doing okay." Harri shrugged. "She and her girlfriend are talking marriage."

"Your advice is I become a lesbian?" A sharp bark of laughter erupted from Monica before she clutched her side and moaned. "That was stupid."

"Do you need something for the pain?"

"No." Monica shook her head and relaxed. "Over-the-counter stuff doesn't do much for me, and I'm past needing something stronger."

Harri doubted that load of crap, but she wasn't licensed to practice medicine. "Eat your breakfast. I've got to get some work done."

"Are you sure Molly's okay working on this show?"

Harri wanted to scream. So much for avoiding talking to her husband's ex today.

"I've got four clients involved in *Make Me a Superhero*," she said. "They are all looking out for each other."

"But Molly's so sweet." Monica sighed. "And let's face it, she's a little gullible. Like I was."

Harri doubted if Monica was ever gullible. Manipulative. Entitled. A little narcissistic. But not gullible.

She crossed her arms. "What do you want me to say, Monica?"

"I—" The supervillain hesitated. "I know you hate my guts, but I also know you want the best for Kerry and Molly, and you won't lie to me."

"I don't hate your guts." Harri sighed. "But you made bad decisions your entire life. It's up to you to change if you want a relationship with your daughters."

"What do you mean change?"

"Stop being a manipulative bitch like your mother for starters."

Monica stared at Harri for a long time before she nodded. "Like I said, you won't lie to me."

Discretion was definitely the better part of valor in this case. "Eat your breakfast, Monica."

Harri retreated to the kitchen before she did something to the supervillain she'd regret.

Like stab Monica's fork through her eyeball.

CHAPTER 22

After finishing her interview segments, Jaye hid in an unused dressing room behind the big theater. She texted Mary where she was before she removed the wig and stripped off her clothing.

By the time Mary arrived, Jeremy was decked out in all black, shoes, socks, trousers, and turtleneck. He towel-dried the sweat from his natural hair. While he'd be wearing a full face ski mask for his interview as Mr. X, Dale said he wanted an unmasked segment for after the big reveal of Jeremy's identity on the show. He'd thrown in a tube of hair gel in his tote to have a modicum of style when Dale's people filmed the post-reveal interview.

"Did you have any problems ditching Sheila?" He packed his Jaye clothes and tote into a duffle bag while Mary opened her cases.

"Nah, she thinks I'm going out to pick up brunch for the makeup department, which I will do as soon as I'm done with you." Mary glanced at his nails. "Please tell me you're wearing gloves. Leo does such a fab job. I hate removing his artwork."

Jeremy examined his hands. Gold curlicues on a turquoise base matched his favorite casual dress. Leonardo knew what it took to make Jaye feel pretty.

"Yes, I brought gloves with me."

"Good." She waved a hand at the folding chair he scrounged. "Now, sit so I can reach your lovely face and totally ruin all the work you did this morning."

Jeremy did as he was told, and Mary removed Jaye's makeup.

She had a gentle touch which was one of the reasons he'd hired her a few years ago. Once his face was clean, she started over again, using a light hand for cis-het male stage makeup.

"Jaye, you sure you want to out your Mr. X persona?" she asked softly.

Mary was the only other person at the salon besides Leonardo who knew about his side hustle. He trusted the two of them to vet any potential clients who aren't referred from a previous customer.

"Are you worried about your safety?" he asked.

"Not with my cousin Kordell living with me." She chuckled. "Without you and your sisters, I don't think he would've stayed on the straight and narrow."

"He did pay you back for rent and groceries, didn't he?"

"Dammit, Jeremy, did you make him feel guilty about that stuff?" Mary held the mascara wand as if she considered poking him in the eye with it.

"That was part of my deal with him," Jeremy said. "I wasn't going to let anyone take advantage of one of my favorite people."

She shook her head. "You're the reason that proverb about fish was created. Now, tilt your head back and look up."

He did as she asked, and she applied the dark brown mascara. "You're comparing me to a stinky fish?"

"You know the one," she murmured. "You don't just serve the fish. You teach people how to fish for themselves. Done."

He straightened his neck and shrugged. "People need to believe in themselves. I've seen too many give up."

"True." Mary sighed and then smiled. "To answer your question, yes, Kordell did pay me back with interest. With the extra money coming in, he's talking about moving all of us into a bigger house."

"Why? Your house is just fine for the three of you."

"He's got his heart set on your sisters getting his baby back for him."

"Whoa!" Jeremy stood. "Harri's going to try but it's not a done deal."

"I know she never gave him any guarantees." Mary began putting her accoutrements back in their cases. "But it wasn't what Kordell wanted to hear. He's been trying so hard to keep his nose clean. I worry about him doing something stupid if Harri does find his son."

"Sweetheart, I doubt if he will do anything stupid," Jeremy said. "He's been bonding with Harri and Tim's foster son, and he's looking forward to spending time with his own kid. Besides, if Kordell does anything stupid to permanently lose his son's custody, Harri will kick his ass long before you get to him."

"I know." Mary snapped the fasteners of the last case. "He's hoping his own boy is getting decent treatment. But you and I both know blood ain't everything. What if his son doesn't want to live with him?"

Jeremy pulled Mary close. "Both Kordell and his son will be fine, and Kordell's not the only one who dotes on Diego." He released her. "Now, go get that food you promised the other makeup peeps."

"Have fun!" She grabbed her cases and strode out of the dressing room.

Jeremy donned his scarlet jacket and waited a few minutes to give her a chance to get back to the main theater section of the building.

It left him too much time to think. He'd been adamant about not having children. Messing up an innocent boy or girl like his parents had screwed him up left him with nightmares.

But Harri had even more pressure on her to have kids between

Eddie and society, which she resisted with all her might. Now, she seemed rather content with Diego living with her and Tim.

Jeremy tugged on the black ski mask. Maybe it was time for him to broach the subject of adopting or fostering a kid or two with Leonardo. There were a lot of good kids like himself who'd simply been given a raw deal in life and needed help. Yep, he'd definitely bring this up over dinner with Leonardo.

Slipping out of the unused dressing room, Jeremy strode up the hallway to the baby theater. He turned the corner to find someone sprawled facedown on the industrial carpet. The brilliant red sneakers sent a trill of alarm through him.

"Vinh!" Jeremy jogged to the kid and crouched next to him. "Vinh, can you hear me?"

When Jeremy didn't get an answer, he dropped his duffle bag and reached for the side of the kid's neck. Nothing. No pulse whatsoever. Nor did he appear to be breathing.

Anger flooded Jeremy. It wasn't the first time he'd found someone like him dead. Darla, one of the queens who'd taken him under their wings twenty-five years ago, committed suicide. Life was hard enough with all the crap thrown at his people.

He reached for his phone in his inside jacket pocket.

"Freeze!"

He looked up to find the security guard Murph pointing a taser at him.

CHAPTER 23

"I just found Vinh," Jeremy said. "Please call 9-1-1."

"Put your hands up," Murph barked.

Jeremy complied. Getting tased right now wouldn't help Vinh one bit.

Murph pulled his radio from his belt. "Base, this is Murphy. I need backup in the connecting hall between the backstage area of the main theater and the baby theater. I also need medical. I've got one man unconscious on the floor. Another man in a black ski mask is crouched over him."

"The kid isn't breathing and there's no heartbeat. You can keep the taser on me, but let me do CPR," Jeremy begged. "Please Murph."

Murph appeared confused. "Lady Jaye?"

"Yeah, I'm also Mr. X, one of the show's judges." Jeremy swallowed hard. "It's supposed to be a secret. Bernhardt wants to do a big reveal during the last episode. I went to the one of the unused dressing rooms to change so none of the crew could see me. I was on my way back to do the cast interview as Mr. X when I found Vinh."

"Just because I know who you are, it doesn't mean you didn't do something to Vinh." Murph pursed his lips a moment before he said, "Do the CPR."

Jeremy slowly lowered his hands and rolled Vinh over to his back.

And nearly lost his breakfast at the sight of a large tempered glass nail file shove through the kid's left eyeball and well into his brain.

"Holy shit," Murph whispered.

Thank goodness, Vinh had been lying face down. The carpet had absorbed what little blood and fluid dripped out of his wound. Jeremy pulled off his mask and sucked in air.

He wasn't sure how long he breathed into Vinh's mouth and pumped his chest. When one of the paramedics gently pushed him out of the way, his arms and ribs ached as he stood. He took a few steps away from the paramedics, sat back against the wall and watched them attempt to save Vinh. But deep down, Jeremy feared it was too late. Sweat trickled down his temples and forehead, ruining Mary's efforts from less than a half hour ago.

Dimly, he heard Murph tell the police it had been fifteen minutes since he discovered Vinh and Jeremy in the hallway. One of the beat cops edged around the paramedics. The hallway was large enough to move props and scenery between the two theaters, but the gurney and equipment were spread out around Vinh. The cop looked down at Jeremy.

"Is it Mr. Jaye or Ms. Jaye?"

"Actually, my legal name is Jeremy Harkness." He closed his eyes against their burning sensation. "Lady Jaye is my stage name."

"Who found Mr. Dang?"

Jeremy forced his eyes open. The cop now held his own cell phone on which he took notes.

"I did."

"How long ago was that?"

One of the paramedics held the defibrilllator paddles. The shiny sheets of metal distracted Jeremy. They cut open Vinh's fashionable top in order to use the device. "Clear!" the paramedic yelled.

The second paramedic leaned away from Vinh. Her partner discharged the paddles before he announced what the EKG machine hummed. "Nothing." The second paramedic continued her chest compressions.

Jeremy shook his head and looked up at the cop questioning him. "I'm not sure. Mary Blu re-did my makeup in an unused dressing room I found. I checked the time on my phone after she left, and it was eleven-forty-five. I left the dressing room about five minutes later."

"Mary Blu?"

"She's a makeup artist and nail tech at Hair Quotes, which I own," Jeremy answered. "Dale Bernhardt, the producer of *Make Me a Superhero*, hired Mary and two other of my employees to work on the show."

The cop frowned. "Bernhardt hired them away from you?"

"No." Jeremy weakly chuckled. "He contracted with my salon manager Elaine Trask for their services."

"Why were you in an unused dressing room instead of one of the ones the production company are using today?"

"Because no one is supposed to know the host Lady Jaye and one of the judges known as Mr. X are the same person. It's one of the big surprise reveals at the end of the season."

The cop shook her head. "Who knows about your dual roles?"

"On the show, only Mr. Bernhardt and Ms. Blu as far as I know," Jeremy answered. "The security guard Murphy learned when I took off the ski mask in order to perform CPR."

"Did Ms. Blu take this hallway when she came back to the dressing room to do your makeup?"

"I'm not sure which route she took. I texted her the location of the dressing room I was in, but I wasn't with her when she came or left." Jeremy's gut clenched as the paramedics did another round with the defibrillator. Still no response from Vinh.

"You left the dressing room and . . . ?" the officer prompted.

"I turned the corner." Jeremy gestured at the cross hallway. "Vinh was facedown on the floor. When he didn't answer me, I crouched next to him. Shook him, then checked for his pulse. When I couldn't find one, I started to reach into my pocket for my phone to call 9-1-1. That's when Murph found us."

"Why were you wearing a ski mask?"

Jeremy winced. He was definitely going to need an attorney. Maybe he should call Susan because he couldn't deal with Harri. Not right now. "So no one would recognize me due to the end-of-show reveal. Like I said, I took it off before I started resuscitation."

"Who rolled over Mr. Dang?"

"I did in order to start CPR."

"Where did that nail file come from?"

"I have no idea. I didn't bring my kit with me because Mary was going to take off my Lady Jaye makeup and do the Mr. X makeup for me." Jeremy took off his left glove, held up his hand, and waggled his fingers. "She didn't touch my nails because she considers my husband the ultimate artist."

To the cop's credit, he didn't make any faces, much less an obnoxious comment. He asked for Jeremy's address and phone number.

"Wait here." The cop stepped aside and muttered something into his shoulder mic.

Meanwhile, the paramedics loaded Vinh onto the gurney with the help of the other police officers. One of the paramedics straddled the kid to continue CPR while the rest of the first responders hustled the gurney up the hall.

The cop turned back to Jeremy. "Mr. Harkness, the techs are on their way to process the scene, including you and Mr. Murphy."

Jeremy nodded. "And then the detectives will want to question me further."

The cop's eyes narrowed. "What were you picked up for?"

"I wasn't." Jeremy shrugged. "One of my former brothers-in-law was a detective with the CPPD before he transferred to the FBI. The other was a prosecutor. I'm just familiar with the drill from more than a few family dinners."

"Do you have a lawyer?" the cop asked.

Jeremy nodded. Harri was going to read him the riot act for touching Vinh, but he couldn't let the kid die without trying to save him. Jeremy closed his eyes again and prayed his foster sister wouldn't have one of their mutual clients drop him in Lake Del Oro to punish him for being stupid.

CHAPTER 24

When Harri's cell phone buzzed, both she and Monica jumped. Luckily, their peanut butter and jelly sandwiches didn't fly off their plates. Harri didn't normally go for horror movies, but if it kept Monica occupied, she'd take it. She just didn't expect to get sucked into the story while they ate lunch.

However, her blood chilled when the main number for the Canyon Pointe Police Department appeared on her caller ID.

"Hello?"

"Harri, I need you to come downtown." Jeremy sounded terrible. In fact, the last time he sounded this bad was when a good friend of his committed suicide twentysome years ago.

She set her plate on her TV tray. "What happened? Are you all right?"

"One of the design contestants for the show is dead." Jeremy's voice caught. "I-I'm the one who found him. The cops are trying to make a case that I killed him."

"Aw, shit." Harri rubbed her forehead. Criminal defense wasn't her specialty, but she'd been doing a hell of a lot of it since she and Aisha started their private practice. "I'm on my way." She ended the call.

"Who's my new baby sitter?" At least, Monica wasn't smirking when she said that. Harri would have decked her if she had.

"You promised Molly you wouldn't leave until she was finished filming *Make Me a Superhero*."

Monica sighed. "You're going to hold me to that?"

"It depends." Harri shrugged. "No one knows you're here outside of the residents of the building, Serena, and Doctor O'Brien. The minute you step outside, Rue Liberty or her people will kill you. The one thing you're good at is self-preservation."

"And you don't want to spend life in prison for aiding and abetting a convicted felon," Monica shot back.

"Not particularly," Harri replied.

"What if I need help before Molly gets home?"

"She's probably on her way home now." Harri stood and collected her plate and glass of diet cola. "The cops shut down the production of *Make Me a Superhero*. One of the contestants was murdered."

By the time Harri changed into a business suit and took the elevator down to the first floor, Molly stood outside the gates of the car.

"Harri, CPPD took Jeremy downtown—"

"He called." Harri pushed open the gates and stepped out of the car. "Tell me what you know."

"No one knows for sure, but the rumor going around the theater is one the security guards found Mr. X next to one of the contestants in a back hallway." Molly shook her head. "Since cast members have been coming and going today, no one knows if it was one of the new supers or one of the designers. Jeremy hasn't been outed as far as I know, but with the police questioning him, it's not going to stay a secret for long."

"Stay with your mom. I'll take care of Jeremy."

Molly blinked. "You left her alone in the loft?"

"I'm holding her to the promise she made to you." Harri smiled. "Besides, she's still having problems getting on and off the toilet."

Molly giggled. "True. Thanks for watching her this morning." She stepped into the car.

"Wait! Was Queen Dazzle still at the theater when they found the body?"

Molly shook her head. "She was one of the first to do interviews. She'd already left for the day."

"Thanks, Molly. I'll stop in and check on you guys when I get back." Harri waved and strode into the main lobby. Behind her, the elevator ground to life.

Janna was on the phone with someone. "Please hold." She jabbed a button. "Harri, Nella Lopez is on the phone. Something about a murder at the Jack Canyon Theater? Do you want to talk to her or should I send her to Susan?"

"Tell Nella I'll call her back in five minutes." Harri tapped her nails on the granite counter while Janna relayed her message and ended the call. "I'm heading down to the police station."

"What's going on?" Susan walked over to them from the break room with a steaming cup of tea.

"I'll explain as I head for the garage." Harri turned back to Janna. "I'm simply out for the afternoon."

Janna rolled her eyes. "Give me a little bit of credit, Harri."

She winced. "I'm sorry I'm taking my nerves out on you. If I'm not back before you have to leave, have a good evening."

Harri headed toward the side exit to the garage with Susan at her side. "Allegedly, one of the cast members of *Make Me a Superhero* was killed this morning. Jeremy's downtown being questioned."

Susan muttered a couple of scathing obscenities before she said, "They're sure it wasn't an accident?"

"I don't know all the details yet," Harri replied. "I'll call you when I do."

"Or you can swing by my place later for a glass of wine?" Susan offered.

"That sounds like a better idea. Thanks." Harri shoved the door open. Hot, muggy air slapped her in the face. By the time she reached her ancient sedan, the back of her neck was quite damp. She was glad she'd taken a few seconds to roll her hair into a bun.

With the A/C on blast, she pulled onto Sixth Street. Overhead, the dark clouds boiled. One of the joys of late winter were the thunderstorms rolling off the mountains west of the city. She prayed she'd make it to the main police station before the rain cut loose.

Harri pressed the speed dial icon for Nella Lopez, the producer for Action 12! News.

"Hey, Harri. Thanks for calling me back." Nella sounded way too happy for someone who learned a person had been murdered. "Can I get a statement from Nix or Queen Dazzle on the designer who was killed at the Jack Canyon Theater?"

"You already know more than either of them at the moment," Harri said. "Nix didn't know who was dead. I was talking to her when you called."

"And?" Nella prompted.

"I'm not holding back on you. I swear."

"Aisha would give me something," Nella grumbled.

"Are you saying my partner lies to you on a regular basis?" Harri snapped.

"No! That's not what I'm saying," Nella protested.

"Good." Harri took a deep breath. "I don't know what's happening yet. Like I said, Nix didn't even know who they found when the cops cleared the theater, and Queen Dazzle had finished filming her preliminary interviews and left for the day."

"You're in your car." Suspicion laced Nella's voice. "Are you headed downtown?"

Harri forced a laugh. "Guilty as charged. But I can honestly say it's not one of my super clients."

"Really?"

"Really."

"Okay." Nella sighed. "I'm sorry I doubted you."

"Look, I know I'm a bitch compared to Aisha, but I also know how important her relationship with your station is to her." Harri swallowed hard. "The last thing I want to do is ruin that relationship. I'm sorry for getting irritated with you. I know you're just doing your job. But honest to god, I'm not holding out on you."

"Thanks, Harri," Nella said. "If I learn anything, I'll let you know. Your clients can take care of themselves, but if there's a murderer wandering around the Jack Canyon . . ."

"Any heads up you can give Nix and Queen Dazzle would be much appreciated."

They said their goodbyes and ended the call as Harri reached downtown proper. Maybe the Big Guy was listening to her prayers for once because she found a spot on the first floor of the parking garage. The first huge drops of rain fell as she yanked open the door at the main entrance of the downtown police station.

It only took a couple of minutes for her to be escorted to the interrogation room where they held Jeremy. The cop left, locking the door behind him.

After hugging her foster brother, Harri perched on the chair next to the one where Jeremy had been sitting. "Tell me everything, starting from when you first arrived at the theater."

She took notes while he told her his version of events. Unfortunately, her desperate wish of this being an accident fell apart when Jeremy told her of the glass nail file shoved through the kid's eyeball and into his brain.

At a knock on the interrogation room door, both she and Jeremy shut up. She was a little surprised when Lloyd Harrison, the chief of police entered. But she had the urge to rip out someone's moustache when she saw the prosecutor.

Calvin Johnson, AKA Aisha's jerk of an ex-husband.

CHAPTER 25

"Hello, Cal," Jeremy said coolly. "A pleasure to see you again, Lloyd."

"This could have been handled by someone else in your departments, gentlemen," Harri said.

At least she wasn't trying to stab Cal with her pen. It was bad enough she egged his car when she found out Cal had cheated on Aisha.

"Harri, please be nice," Jeremy murmured. "I really don't want to spend the night in jail."

"It won't be like my night," Harri snarled. "Black Death is in prison this time."

"If you two are finished?" Cal said dryly. He sat on the other side of the table. The police chief remained standing.

Harri opened her mouth. Jeremy kicked her under the table. Her jaw snapped shut, and she glared at him.

"Please continue, Mr. Johnson," Jeremy said.

"*Ese*, why the hell were you running around in a black ski mask?" Cal said.

Jeremy sighed. "It's part of the show. My identity as a judge is supposed to be a secret until the final episode. Like I told one of the responding officers, I was in one of the dressing rooms for the main theater, changing my clothes for the personal profiles they're shooting today."

He turned to Harri. "I told you exactly what I said to the officer. Any problem repeating this stuff to Cal."

Harri pursed her lips and shook her head. The girl needed to let go of her anger at Aisha's ex. Their foster sister was happily married to a superhero hunk, and they had an adorable baby. But Harri seemed to take Cal's betrayal so personally, even though it was five years ago.

Jeremy repeated his story to Cal and Lloyd. When he finished, the two men exchanged looks.

"Your story matches Ms. Blu's and Mr. Murphy's," Lloyd said.

"Which means you're all innocent, or you're all in this together," Cal added.

"But what's the motive?" Harri demanded. "Jeremy only met the victim this morning."

"Unless Mr. Dang saw him without his mask if keeping his identity secret was a major element of the show." Cal tapped his pen on the legal pad in front of him.

"Have you checked for prints on the weapon?" Harri asked.

"Yes, but Mr. Harkness was wearing gloves when he was discovered with the victim," Lloyd said.

Harri crossed her arms. "So, all you have is an out-of-his-depth, rent-a-cop, post-murder witness and circumstantial evidence?"

At Cal's sheepish look, Harri snorted. "Call me if you have any further questions for my client." She stood. "C'mon, Jeremy. Let's go home."

He eyed Cal. "I may have only met Vinh this morning, but he was a good kid, working his butt off to make something of his life. He didn't deserve what was done to him."

"*Ese*, tell your producer he might want to put up security cameras all over the theater." Cal shook his head. "I was surprised to find out he didn't have any cameras anywhere else in the theater. I thought all these reality shows liked filming the so-called private moments."

"He might take it more seriously if it comes from you, Cal." Jeremy headed for the door.

Lloyd cleared his throat.

"Yeah, yeah, yeah. I don't need the lecture about leaving Canyon Pointe." Jeremy opened the door and stalked out of the interrogation room.

Harri made him stop long enough to grab his things and sign for them. As he and Harri stared at the rain from the main entrance of the police station, she asked, "You wanna hit Java Joe's?"

"No." Jeremy's shoulders sagged. He'd gotten up way too early for such a shitty day. "I do have half a mind to drink all of La Churro's tequila supply."

"Did Vinh remind you of you?"

He glanced at Harri. She watched him with a worried expression.

"No." He shook his head. "Vinh is, was, way smarter than I was at his age. He was going to give Sabrina a run for her money in this competition. I don't get why someone would kill him. It doesn't make sense."

"Would you object if I turn Tim and Arthur loose?"

"Are you kidding me?" Jeremy checked around them. The desk sergeant was giving him an odd look, but no one else cared. "How close is your car?"

"There." She pointed at the garage across the street. The rear end of her Accord was just visible from where they stood.

"It's that close, and we're standing here like a couple of dummies?"

She smirked. "Then let's go."

It didn't take much to talk Harri into some food at La Churro's, especially after she admitted all she had was half of a peanut butter sandwich for lunch. The place was nearly empty this late in the afternoon. And despite his threat at the police station, he ordered an ice tea, and Harri ordered a diet soda.

Mateo shot them both worried looks before he headed back to the bar.

Harri pulled out her phone. "Tell me what you can about this Vinh Dang."

"Twenty. Vietnamese-American. He's attending the University of Colorado in Boulder." Jeremy raked his hand through his hair. It was hard to pull their conversation out of his memory when all he saw was that blasted nail file thrust through the kid's head. "He'd been to Lady Jaye's Revue, and he asked for my autograph, but he asked to wait until after the production wrapped. His roommate in Boulder is originally from Canyon Pointe. She brought him to the Revue."

Harri typed the info into her phone. "Could the roommate have come with him to Canyon Pointe?"

Jeremy frowned. "It's the middle of the semester. I doubt if she would have. But he may have been staying with her family during filming. None of us were rich when we were in school."

"Ain't that the truth." Harri grimaced. "Anything else you can thing of?"

"His clothes were off the rack, but altered. The most expensive thing he wore were his designer high tops. Brilliant red."

Harri typed in Jeremy's description, then whistled. "Are these the ones?" She turned her phone so he could see the screen.

He nodded. "Yep, Buck Supe's line."

"How could a college student afford some very expensive shoes with a rapper's name?" Harri turned the phone to look at the shoes again.

"Maybe they were a gift." Jeremy shrugged. "Your grandmother would give me clothes like that when we were kids."

"I remember." Harri smiled. "You were the fashion-interested grandchild she wished she had. Let the boys do some digging." She put her phone away. "If they come up with anything, I'll let you know. Did the cops say how long before you guys will be allowed back into the Jack Canyon?"

"No, but I'm sure Bernhardt's bitching up a storm." Jeremy sipped his ice tea. "He's losing money with this kind of delay. Then there's the bad publicity when the press gets ahold of the story."

"They already do," Harri admitted. "Nella called the office as I was leaving to get you. She wanted a statement from Nix or Queen Dazzle. At that point, Nella knew more than the supers or I did about what happened."

Jeremy stared at her. "Please tell me my name didn't come up."

"Give me a little credit," Harri said dryly.

"Have you called Leonardo?" he asked.

"Not my spouse, not my news."

Jeremy hated to admit she was right. But he dreaded the conversation. Leonardo was going to have a major fit when he found out what happened at the theater.

CHAPTER 26

An hour later, Jeremy's fear came true when he and Harri entered his loft. "Hi, baby doll."

Leonardo jumped off the stool at the breakfast bar and stalked over to them. "Where the hell have you been?"

"The police station and La Churro's—" Jeremy began.

"La Churro's? After someone was murdered?"

"Calm down, baby doll—"

"I'm pissed because I had to hear it on the radio at the salon!" Red suffused Leonardo's face. "Why didn't you call me?"

Jeremy winced. It wasn't often Leonardo lost his temper, but when he did, he made all the queens at the Revue look like they were on Xanax.

"Because I was allowed one call, and I needed a lawyer to get me the hell out of a locked interrogation room." Jeremy took a deep breath to calm himself. "They were trying to pin Vinh's murder on me because I found him. I wasn't trying to hide anything from you. But I needed Harri to deal with the mess. If I called you, what would you have done, baby doll?"

"Call Harri," Leonardo admitted. "You don't know how scared I was when that news report came on. It could have been you who was dead."

"Oh, god, I didn't even think of that." Jeremy pulled his husband into his arms. "I'm so, so sorry."

Gradually, the tension left Leonardo's body, and he sniffed. "Please don't do that to me again."

"The La Churro's thing was my fault, Leo," Harri said. "Jaye needed some time to process what happened. I didn't think it was fair to dump him on you."

Leonardo stepped back and gave Harri the evil eye. "You could have called me. Let me know you were on your way, and my husband was alive."

She glared right back. "I'll remember that the next time you get married and don't invite me."

"You're still holding that over our heads?" Jeremy threw his arms in the air.

"Only when you two yell at me for doing my job." Harri crossed her arms. "Jaye, have you considered the possibility that someone knows you're Mr. X and is trying to frame you?"

His blood chilled at Harri's suggestion. "This is why I've kept my identity a secret!"

"Is there an unhappy customer you've cut ties with?" Damn, she was like terrier with a rat. "A supervillain you offended by not designing a supersuit for them?"

Jeremy nodded slowly. "Back when I first started designing. If it weren't for Mel, a couple of supervillains would have killed me."

"You never told me this," Leonardo exclaimed.

"Don't feel bad, Leo," Harri muttered. "Jaye's hid a lot of shit from me, too. Does Aisha know about this?"

"No, she doesn't," Jeremy snapped. "No one but the two idiots and Mel know."

"Who was it?" Harri reached into her jacket pocket for her phone once again. "We can track them down. Make sure they aren't behind this."

"They called themselves Scorpion Sting and Red Widow, the king and queen of crime."

Harri frowned. "They don't sound familiar. When did this go down?"

God, this was so embarrassing, but she was right. They needed to track down any potential lead in Vinh's death.

"It'll be seventeen years this July," Jeremy admitted.

"That's what really happened to you that night?" Harri stared at him.

"What happened?" Leonardo wore a concerned expression.

"It was after the Ryan fiasco," Harri growled. "Your idiot husband was drinking too much and picking up any guy willing to do him. Aisha had moved in with Cal, but I was still living with him. He came home from an alleged Fourth of July party at Purple Eggplant, sporting a couple of shiners, scrapes on his knuckles, and a missing tooth. And that's only what I saw. The butthead wouldn't let me take him to the ER or call the police. He claimed it was a couple of bigoted asshats who jumped him outside of the club."

"I didn't lie," Jeremy protested. "Scorpion Sting and Red Widow were bigoted asshats who jumped me outside of the Eggplant."

"You left out the supervillain part." Harri closed her eyes and rubbed the spot between her eyebrows with her middle finger.

"Geez, Harri," Jeremy muttered. "Subtle much."

She lowered her hand and opened her eyes. "Do you have any appointments with any of your salon clients over the rest of the month?"

"Yeah, a snotty lawyer who needs her roots done," he bit back.

"I can handle Harri's touch-ups," Leonardo said. "He cleared his calendar for filming the show, other than your salon appointment and revamping Nix's look."

"I'm not hiding in our loft!" Jeremy bellowed. He'd worked too damn hard to accept himself. He'd worked too damn hard to support his community. And he worked too damn hard to build his businesses.

"I didn't throw temper tantrums when Seismic Shit and Corvus were trying to kill me," Harri muttered.

Jeremy stared at her for a good long time. Good grief, she really believed her BS. He turned to look at Leonardo and couldn't help himself at his hubby's smirk. They both broke up laughing.

"Hey!" Harri literally stomped her foot. "Stop it!"

Her act only made Jeremy and Leonardo laugh harder. Harri's nostrils flared, and her cheeks turned neon pink. And for a tiny woman, she had a wicked right cross. Jeremy worked to get his mirth under control.

"All right, all right." He waved his hands. "I'm sorry. I'll lay low for the next twenty-four hours. Will that be enough time for Timmy and Arthur to do their thing?"

"Don't take your car—" She stopped with a confused expression. "Wait. Where is your car?"

"Unless the police impounded it during their investigation, it's probably still sitting in the back parking lot at the Jack Canyon," Jeremy said.

"Here." Harri grabbed his hand and slapped her keys into his palm. "Use my sedan. Your red convertible is too noticeable. Tim and I can swing by and pick it up."

"I guess I should be grateful you're not insisting I drive Aisha's rugrat-mobile." Jeremy sighed. "How are you planning to get home?"

But Harri was already texting. "Dopinder's on his way. We'll keep your baby on the second floor of our garage. Are you going to object if I hire someone as your bodyguard?"

"Hell, yes." Jeremy rattled her keys in her face. "You are blowing this out of proportion."

"Jaye, there's a kid lying in the morgue." Harri turned terribly serious. "We have no idea who killed him or why. Until we do, you need to watch your back. And before you go full queen on me, I'm giving the same lecture to Sabrina, Nix, and Dazzle. I don't want to—I can't lose you guys. Especially you."

Tears glimmered in Harri's eyes. While she was handling Aisha being in Paris fairly well, her abandonment issues were on full display. Jeremy pulled her into his arms and tried to send reassurance through his hug.

"I promised to play it your way for tomorrow," he whispered.

Her phone buzzed, and he released her. She blinked rapidly to keep her tears from falling while she checked her message.

"Dopinder's downstairs," she murmured.

Jeremy handed her the keys to his baby before he gave her another hug for good measure. Leonardo embraced her, then she whirled and left without another word.

"I'm glad you're listening to her." Leonardo wrapped an arm around Jeremy's waist. "I don't think I've ever seen her scared."

"She hides a lot of what she really feels." Jeremy shook his head. "But not so much anymore. Not since she and Timmy hooked up."

Leonardo looked up at Jeremy with narrowed eyes. "And if you even think of sneaking out tomorrow, I will call Tim and have him tie you to our bed if that's what it takes to keep you safe."

"Promises, promises," Jeremy teased.

The last thing he wanted to do was scare Leonardo, but this whole situation bothered him more than he wanted to admit.

Why on earth would someone target an innocent twenty-year-old kid?

CHAPTER 27

After Dopinder dropped Harri off at the Lechuza Building, she marched straight to Susan's office and relayed the events at the theater and the police station. Harri apologized for passing on the wine and a little girl talk tonight since she hadn't gotten a damn thing done this afternoon. Thankfully, Susan didn't appear to hold it against Harri.

She then checked in on Molly and Monica. For the first time since Monica got back on her feet, the mother and daughter weren't arguing. Harri told Molly as much as she could about Vinh Dang's death.

When Harri stood to head back to her own loft, Monica said, "Aren't you forgetting something?"

Harri sighed. "What am I forgetting?"

"Aren't you going to tell her to be careful?" Monica scowled at Harri. "There's a murderer running around that production, and it sounds like the police don't have a freakin' clue."

"No, I'm not because I trust your daughter to watch her back." Harri smirked. "And I believe in her judgment a whole lot more than I believe in yours."

Monica's mouth dropped open, but Harri didn't wait for a sarcastic remark from the supervillain. She left and stalked across the hall to her own loft. She slid open the door to discover Diego and Javi playing Foxstar.

"Homework?" she growled.

Once again, mouths dropped open.

She closed her eyes. Maybe it was a good thing she'd never gotten pregnant.

"Uh, I'll see you later, D."

Harri opened her eyes in time to see Javi dart out her front door. She rolled it shut and eyed Diego.

"Do I need to repeat the rules here?"

"No." Diego put the controllers back in the little cupboard on the TV stand. "And my homework is done."

"What about studying for your earth science test tomorrow?"

"I know that stuff. I'm ready for it," he protested.

"Good." Harri smiled. "Let me change, and I'll quiz you while we prep for dinner."

An expression of horror washed over the teenager. "Tim's not cooking tonight?"

"Before you have a total panic attack, he left us instructions for one of his sheet pan meals.

"Those are pretty good, but can we please have potatoes instead of cauliflower rice?"

"I was thinking the same thing, D." She winked at him before she headed to her bedroom. Tim's low carb diet was fine for someone turning fifty this year, but a growing kid needed a more well-rounded meal once in a while.

Diego had set the table while she donned jeans and a t-shirt. Instead of plain broiled chicken, she mixed up Tim's crunchy cheddar topping for the breasts and quizzed Diego from his notes and textbook on his iPad while he diced the potatoes. Once the first round was in the oven, she perched on one of their stools with a glass of wine and continued with the questions while Diego washed and prepped the broccoli for the second baking sheet. By the time he popped the vegetables into the oven, too, she had to admit the kid was ready for his test.

Diego grabbed a bottle of orange juice from the refrigerator and sat on the stool next to Harri. "Is Jeremy okay?"

"Yes. Why?"

"The murder at the J.C. was all over the news, and—" Diego swallowed hard. "Javi and I accidentally overheard Tim and Arthur talking about Jeremy being questioned by the police."

Harri hesitated. While she trusted her foster brother with her life, there was always the possibility Diego's parents would use Jeremy's lifestyle and extracurricular activities against her.

"He's fine, just very upset," she finally said. "He was the one who found the dead person."

"Oooo! Yuck!" Diego winced. "Was it totally gross?"

"Can we not talk about corpses right before dinner?"

"I'm worried about my dad, too," Diego admitted. "He got a job as a guard at the theater, and he hasn't answered any of my texts this afternoon."

Harri laid her palm on Diego's shoulder. "I can guarantee the victim was not your dad."

"Can you call him?" the kid asked in a very soft voice.

"I technically can't because I represent you." Harri picked up her phone from the breakfast bar. "However, I can call your dad's attorney." She tapped the contact icon for Lisa Ashcraft's cell phone.

"What did Isla Murphy do this time?" Lisa ground out.

"Hello, Lisa," Harri said cheerfully, hoping the other attorney would take the hint. "Diego's been trying to reach his dad today. I don't know if you heard about the body that was found at the Jack Canyon Theater. Diego says Carl got a job down there, and he's worried about his dad."

"We both just left the theater," Lisa said. "I drove him down to pick up his car after he was questioned by the detectives assigned to the case. Tell Diego I'm sure his dad will call him as soon as he recharges his phone. The battery was dead when I got to the police station."

"My client will be relieved to know that." Harri gave Diego a thumbs up.

"By the way, my client's car wasn't the only one still in the Jack Canyon's back lot," Lisa said. "Jeremy's convertible was parked back there, too."

"Lady Jaye is hosting the show they're filming there," Harri admitted. "Jeremy was the one who found the body."

Lisa's exhalation whistled through the receiver. "That's what Carl said. He also mentioned the circumstances. Is everything okay with him?"

Harri rolled her eyes, even though Lisa couldn't see her expression. "You know Cal Johnson. Anything to harass his ex's family."

Lisa chuckled. "The guy's a weasel. I never understood what Aisha saw in him."

Harri bit her tongue. No good would come from trashing Cal. Not with Jeremy's reputation on the line.

"Thanks for letting me know Carl's all right—"

"Wait! Don't hang up," Lisa blurted. "I've got something related to the Murphy case to ask you."

Harri's muscles tensed. "Go ahead."

"Carl has tickets to the final taping, and he'd like to take Diego. If it's all right with you," Lisa said tentatively.

"That's up to Diego, and that's assuming the production doesn't collapse under the bad publicity," Harri said.

"I thought any publicity was good," Lisa quipped.

"Really? What's Skyball's stock these days?" Harri shot back.

Lisa laughed. "He should have taken a page from Captain Terrific's book and hired Winters and Franklin to represent him."

"Hey, thanks for the update," Harri said.

"No problem." Lisa was still chuckling to herself when she ended the call.

"Your dad's fine. His phone battery died while the police were questioning him, too." Harri set aside her own phone. "Ms. Ashcraft took him back to the theater to pick up his car, and they both left at the same time. If he plugged in his phone to recharge—"

Diego's phone warbled a little tune, and he looked at the screen. "Speak of the devil."

"Go talk to your dad." Harri smiled. "I'll keep dinner warm for us."

The kid jumped off his stool, grabbed his phone, and took off for his bedroom.

Later that night after Diego went to bed, Harri worked on a couple of contracts in her home office when she heard the security system beep. She rose and stretched before she left her office and strolled out to the kitchen.

Tim shut the microwave door and pressed the buttons to warm his dinner. He turned toward her.

And irritation immediately swelled within her at the sight of orange powder on his lips and chin.

"Next time, wipe the Cheetos dust off your mug before you come upstairs," she grumbled.

"What if I brought you the rest of the bag?" He reached for something behind him on the counter and held up a bright orange and blue package.

"Puffs!" Harri squealed. "Gimme!" She lunged for the treats, but he held them up out of her reach.

"Keep it down," he teased. "You'll wake Diego, and we'll have to share with him."

"We owe him some junk food." Harri jumped for the bag and snagged it. "No kid thrives on fake meat and fake rice."

"He's not the one whose health I really worry about." Tim poured a glass of ice tea for himself.

"So says the bionic man." She yanked the clip off the bag and crammed a couple of cheese puffs into her mouth. "Whad oo fine owd?"

The microwave dinged, and Tim removed his plate. "Not much." He grabbed a set of silverware before he headed for their dining table and sat. "Vinh Dang's only arrest was during the LGBT+ rights march in D.C. two years ago. Straight A student. His family was accepting of him from the beginning. He was never in the closet."

Harri swallowed her mouthful of puffs, grabbed a seltzer water, and joined him at the dining table with the remaining Cheetos. "What about his roommate?"

"Dana Meadowfield."

Harri's stomach lurched. "Meadowfield?"

"Yep, Ted and Holland's youngest daughter."

Harri had the urge to beat her head against the tabletop. Dana's father was the former primetime anchor at Action 12! News before he went off the deep end and tried to shoot up Harri and Tim's wedding on New Year's Eve.

CHAPTER 28

"Could she have killed Vinh to frame Jeremy?" Harri stared at her husband.

"Dana has a pretty solid alibi," Tim said. "She's interning at the Fiske Planetarium in Boulder this term. They had a sixth grade overnight event. The police in Boulder have already talked to her and the other adults. They all confirm she never left the planetarium." He forked a piece of broccoli into his mouth and chewed it.

"Jeremy wasn't sure, but he had the feeling Vinh was staying with his roommate's family," Harri said.

Tim nodded and swallowed. "He was. CPPD has spoken with Holland Riggs-Meadowfield. She confirmed it and allowed the detectives to search his room and the rest of the house. They didn't find anything remotely suspicious."

"What about Ted?" Harri asked.

"He's still in the Clark County jail awaiting trial." Tim sipped his tea. "By the way, Holland filed for divorce. It'll hit the media in the morning."

"Everybody's been expecting that for the last two months." Harri grabbed another puff and popped it into her mouth.

"What was more interesting was the idiots down at lockup tossed Gentleman Jim into the same cell as Ted," Tim stated.

Harri stared at him. "You don't think that psycho killed Vinh, do you?"

Tim shook his head as he cut up his chicken breast. "He was

transferred to Mauvaises three days later, but he and Ted are now penpals."

"And?" Harri prompted.

Tim shrugged. "I don't believe it has anything to do with Vinh's death, but it's something we need to keep an eye on. Ted is almost as crazy as Gentleman Jim."

"Almost?"

"The only difference is the level of competence," Tim declared. "Not to be morbid, but if Jim hated you with Ted's passion, we'd all be dead. I just found the county jail's eff-up of putting a known supervillain in a cell with a civilian to be amusing."

Harri leaned back in her chair. "This is making less and less sense."

"Arthur and I will keep digging tomorrow," Tim assured her.

"Yeah, but what are we missing?" Harri reached for another cheese puff.

"I'm going to switch the conversation to our other big project." Tim wiped his mouth with his napkin. "Is Susan up to another visit with Special Agent Consuelo?"

Harri winced. "You need to be the one to ask her."

Tim groaned. "What did you do this time?"

"She asked me to stop by her place for a glass of wine tonight, and I originally said yes. But then the crap with Jeremy hit the fan, and I asked for a raincheck to catch up on work from this afternoon and because Diego needs my attention more than she does—"

"Harri." Tim grabbed her hand that was waving a puff. "I believe you. Take her out to Nolan's for girls' time tomorrow night, and I'll hit her up when you two get home."

She released the rest of the air in her lungs. How'd she get so lucky in marrying Tim?

"Sorry for thinking I need to take care of everything," she murmured. "I'm working on that."

"I know you are." He squeezed her hand. "Let me finish dinner, and we'll find a way to get your mind off your rough day."

"Why Tim Canyon are you trying to seduce me?"

He grinned. "I rather hope I'm succeeding."

Thankfully, when Miguel and his crew converted the fifth floor into living space, he added extra storage space above the bedrooms and soundproofed the walls. Harri and Tim didn't have to worry about waking their ward. Harri deliberately ignored the fact that a handful of people living in the Lechuza Building had superhearing.

When she stopped and asked Susan about going to Nolan's on her way down to the office the next morning, Susan surprised her with an enthusiastic yes.

Harri bit the bullet and said, "Think you can handle feeding Consuelo more information?"

"Hey, if Nolan's peanut butter pie is included tonight, I'll do almost anything you ask." Susan grinned as she locked up her own apartment. "Do I get to take the files Tim stole to her?"

"Actually, you're taking some of the pictures and documents from Grandma Harri's storage locker," Harri said.

"The originals?"

They walked to the elevator.

"Nope, copies you made when I was out of the building over the last couple of days." Harri slid back the gates of the elevator.

"Wow, I'm good at being a double agent." Susan chuckled. "When?"

"This morning?" Harri suggested. "Just so I don't find out you made copies of my grandmother's paperwork."

"Where did I hide the copies I made?"

"In the Owl's Nest." Harri grinned. "You're going down to retrieve them now."

"Damn, I'm good! Hiding them in a dead vigilante's lair. No one would think to look there!" Susan's sarcasm was thicker than Aunt Queenie's sorghum syrup.

Harri scowled at her partner. "That was a step too far."

"Sorry, boss." But Susan kept grinning. "I couldn't help it."

"No, I owe you an apology." Harri sighed as the elevator continued its downward grind. "If it weren't for the murder at the Jack Canyon yesterday, I'd be laughing along with you."

Susan sobered. "I take it Tim and Arthur have no leads."

"Not when they quit for the night around midnight." Harri shook her head. "The police only have circumstantial evidence on Jeremy, and not even much of that, truth be told."

"I know you're afraid they're going to railroad your brother," Susan said softly. "But Chief Harrison, Mayor Benevides, and even Cal have done their best to clean up their respective offices."

"But I've made enough enemies over the years," Harri said. "It wouldn't surprise me if that's the reason Jeremy was in the wrong place at the wrong time."

"Just because Tim and Arthur didn't find anything in the first twelve hours, it doesn't mean they won't find something," Susan assured Harri.

But as they exited the elevator car in the basement, Harri wondered if Jeremy hadn't made a few enemies of his own over the years. Maybe she needed to call Ultramegaperson and have a little girl-to-girl chat with the superhero.

CHAPTER 29

A week later, Jeremy got the call from Bernhardt's assistant that filming would resume in the Jack Canyon Theater the next day. He needed to be at the baby theater at five a.m. for make-up since they were going to film the reveal interview first. Then he could mask up for the other segments.

It was a bit of relief. While he hadn't exactly feared he'd be released from his contract because he had the misfortune of finding Vinh's body, he did worry there'd be no one to watch the backs of the other three girls represented by Winters and Franklin. He'd no sooner ended the call when Leonardo knocked on Jeremy's open home office door.

"We have company, babe."

"Who—" Jeremy started before Mel poked their head over Leonardo's.

"Morning, sugar." They grinned. "I hear you've been causing trouble for my love bug."

Jeremy rose and crossed the room. "Not me. But what are you doing here? Why didn't you call to say you were coming?"

They hugged him, careful not to break his spine with their superstrength. And they made a point not to hug for an excessively long time in front of Leonardo.

When they parted, Mel pursed their green lip-sticked mouth. "I could say I flew out to see Dale, but I've never lied to you and I'm not about to start. Harri called me."

"Harri?" Jeremy placed his hand on his chest in mock dismay. "As in my foster sister Harriet Matilda Winters?"

"Don't be mad, sugar. She's worried about you."

Jeremy shook his head. "What did she say? And I hope you cross-checked everything with your man candy."

"That's why I already asked Leonardo if I can stay in your guest room." Mel shook their head. "If I stay with Dale, he won't get any work done, and I won't be able to keep an eye on you like I promised Harri."

Jeremy opened his mouth to protest, but Mel laid their white-gloved index finger across his lips.

"We need to talk, Jaye. She also called to ask me if you had any run-ins with your former clients."

Jeremy propped his fists on his hips. "What did you tell her?"

"Don't get pissy with me, little girl." Mel waggled their finger in his face. "I'm not the one who hid my profession from your family." Mel lowered their hand. "And I didn't say anything. She already knew about Scorpion Sting and Red Widow. I told her I needed to talk to you first."

"That's because I told her about them," Jeremy grumbled.

"But you didn't tell her about Gentleman Jim, did you?" Mel cocked a perfectly plucked eyebrow and tilted their head.

Crap. That man wasn't your average everyday supervillain. He was a psychotic, serial-killing supervillain.

"I have enough nightmares about him, thank you very much." Jeremy glared at Mel, but they wouldn't take the hint.

"Gentleman Jim?" Leonardo choked out. "He wanted you to design for him?"

"No, baby doll." Jeremy grimaced. "He wanted me to die for him."

"It was a pick-up gone very wrong." Mel's expression turned

sad. "If I hadn't come to Canyon Pointe a day early for my super-suit fitting, you would never have met your spouse, Leonardo."

He crossed his arms and glared at Jeremy. "Is that the real reason you hooked up with Timmy? To cover your ass when Mel wasn't in town?"

"It's the reason I design for nearly every superhero in a five-state radius around Mojave," Jeremy admitted. "And I don't design for any supervillains."

"You need to tell Harri what happened." Mel scowled at him. "Shoving a nail file into someone's brain—"

"Is not his style," Jeremy responded. "He likes to torture people before he kills them, sweetheart."

"Babe, this could very easily be a hate crime." Leonardo shook his head. "You know Harri's boys are going to be picking this Vinh's murder apart, but it's not all about you. There's Nix, Queen Dazzle, and Sabrina involved."

"Dazzle's part of this show?" Mel narrowed their eyes. "Dale forgot to mention that little tidbit."

"Jealous much," Jeremy teased.

"At least, I know you aren't designing for that bitch," Mel spat.

"Our tastes are too different," Jeremy replied, praying silently they would drop the subject.

Unfortunately, God wasn't up to answering prayers today. "They didn't used to be," Mel shot back.

"I'm going down to the salon." Leonardo pivoted and stalked out of the office.

"Sweetcakes, wait." Jeremy rushed after him.

Leonardo turned around, but there was no anger on his face. "Babe, we both have pasts, but if I wanted to waste my day with bitchy queens, I'd be spending more time at the Revue."

"I apologize," Jeremy said. "I didn't mean to drive you out of our home."

"I know." Leonardo sighed. "But for what it's worth, I think Mel's right. You need to have a heart-to-heart with Harri. Vinh died in a horrible way, and the person who did it is still on the loose. She needs every scrap of information to feed to her boys. Unless you want her to call Aisha. Or is that your real plan? Force Aisha to come home because you miss that adorable little nephew of ours?"

Jeremy ran a hand through his hair. Was he really that selfish? Sure, he missed Aisha, Rey, and little Mitch. Or was it something he was afraid of confessing to the man he loved?

"It's more that I don't want you to think less of me," Jeremy said softly. "I'm not trying to impress Mel, but I do care about your opinion of me. And two decades have shown how stupid I was back then."

The corner of Leonardo's mouth quirked. "But you also care about Harri's opinion of you, which is why you haven't told her the truth either. Call her, and see if she can fit you in today. Or invite her, Timmy, and Diego over for dinner tonight."

"How'd I ever get lucky enough to find you?" Jeremy smiled.

"I was right under your nose the whole time." Leonardo rose on his toes and gave Jeremy a kiss that took his breath away. "Call me if you decide to have them over. I need to do a little shopping in Chinatown."

Jeremy watched him saunter down the hallway. Whatever good feelings remained from that kiss bled away under the memory of the night he met Gentleman Jim. And as much as he hated to admit it, both Mel and Leonardo were right about coming clean with Harri.

CHAPTER 30

Jeremy's invitation to dinner at his and Leo's loft took Harri by surprise. Even more so when he said Ultramegaperson was in town and staying with them. Harri half-expected a meltdown from Jeremy for meddling in his life. Or maybe Ultramegaperson handled the situation with more finesse than Harri gave them credit for.

Regardless, it didn't take much convincing for Diego to give the dinner plans an enthusiastic thumbs up when he got home from school. Sometimes, Harri wondered if the real reason Diego wanted to stay with her and Tim was to meet other supers. The kid claimed he didn't want to join the underwear brigade, but he never turned down an opportunity to meet any of her clients with powers. When Harri went down to the Owl's Nest computer lab to tell Tim about the change in dinner plans, her husband groaned.

"Please tell me the guys aren't doing takeout from La Churro's."

"What's wrong with La Churro's?" Harri demanded.

"I'd like to keep my arteries for another couple of decades," he grumbled. "Yours and Jeremy's are already clogged with that goo Mateo calls cheese."

Harri crossed her arms. "Jeremy would have told me if he was serving La Churro's tonight."

Tim crossed his arms and leaned back in his office chair. "Nolan's?"

"You like Nolan's," she protested.

"Not for every meal."

"Why are you complaining?" Harri shook her head. "It means you don't have to cook tonight."

He watched her with narrowed eyes. "Who's cooking then?"

"I didn't ask." She glared right back. "What's really going on?"

Tim held up his hands, fingers spread. "Look, I'm not trying to disparage your brother, but for a gay man, he can't cook worth spit."

"That is an incredibly bigoted and stereotyped thing to say, and you are damn lucky Aisha and Rey aren't here. You might find yourself hanging from the Del Oro Bank's primary antenna."

Harri's mental hamster finally jumped on its wheel. Tim normally wasn't this clueless, which meant something else was going on. She decided to put her theory to the test.

"Well, you can fix yourself fish and seaweed, and Diego and I will go join my family for dinner," she retorted.

She pivoted to leave the computer lab when Tim blurted, "All right. Fine. I'm worried about you and Diego being in the line of fire if someone's really targeting Jeremy."

So, that was it. Flashbacks to when Seismic Shift killed his first wife Rebecca and their son Shane. Harri released the breath she held and turned to face Tim again.

"Honey, that's why Ultramegaperson is in town, and why they're staying at Jeremy and Leo's rather than with their boyfriend Dale at his hotel." She stepped closer and cupped Tim's cheek. "You keep telling me you won't leave me when my own feelings of abandonment make me say stupid things. So, let me do the same. I will never, ever, put Diego in harm's way, and you know damn well Jeremy wouldn't either."

She sighed. "I know that doesn't totally take away your fear, but please don't pick fights with me or insult my remaining family over your own issues." She bent over and kissed Tim lightly on the lips. When she straightened, she added, "If you really don't want to go, that's all right, but I'm trying to show Diego that suiting up is his choice."

Tim grabbed her right hand and kissed her palm. "I'm sorry for acting like an idiot. I didn't realize it until you pointed it out."

Harri chuckled. "When did we switch places?"

Tim laughed. "I think it was the night of our wedding when you took out Ted Meadowfield with a toy gun in front of a half dozen supers."

"Does that mean you'll go to Jeremy and Leo's for dinner?"

"Yes, ma'am." Tim tugged her into his lap for a more thorough apology.

Harri didn't want to admit it to Tim, but his concerns about her brother's culinary abilities were valid. Jeremy could barely handle a cup of noodles in a microwave when they were in school. And his skills hadn't improved since then.

But then, her own kitchen talents sucked, which was why on the nights when Aisha didn't cook when they lived together, the three of them went to La Churro's.

Thankfully, Leo was in charge of dinner tonight. Their loft smelled divine when Harri and her immediate family arrived. Diego promptly started asking Ultramegaperson a zillion questions regarding their exploits. The kid also pulled a pristine copy of *Ultramegaperson #1* out of the backpack he insisted on bringing with him.

"Where did you get that?" Harri knew how much those were going for on the second-hand market. For a split-second, she feared Diego had stolen it.

"It's my bio dad's." The kid carefully pulled the comic out of its protective plastic sheath. "He gave it to me when he found out I had powers." Diego looked at Ultra. "Would you sign it so I can give it back to him? It would mean a lot to him since he's a big fan of yours."

"Sweetheart, your father gave that to you for a reason," Ultra said gently.

"But he gave it to me for the wrong reason," Diego answered. "He was hoping to inspire me to suit up because that's what he would do if our positions were reversed. But he'd really like it if it were signed by you. Plus he got me signed photos of Nix and Queen Dazzle at his new job."

Harri exchanged looks with Tim who appeared as confused as she felt. "When did your dad get a new job?"

"About a month ago," Diego replied while Jeremy brought in soft drinks for their guests. "He's working at the Jack Canyon Theater."

One of the glasses slipped through Jeremy's hand. With their superspeed, Ultra caught it without spilling a drop.

"You okay, Jaye?" Harri asked.

"Is he the head of security at the Jack Canyon?" Jeremy asked in a weird voice.

Diego nodded enthusiastically before he turned serious. "Don't worry, dude. I can keep a secret. I didn't say a thing about you being the lady host. Though Dad said you had great legs." A mischievous grin lit up the kid's face.

"Wait." Harri grabbed her glass of diet cola before Jeremy dropped that one, too. "The security guard who found you with the body was Carl Murphy?"

"I haven't had a chance to find out Murph's first name." Jeremy shivered and dropped onto the chair beside her. "Can it be just a coincidence?"

"There's no such thing as a coincidence when it comes to you and your siblings," Tim muttered.

"Whoa! Dad was there when you found the dead guy?" Diego's eyes widened.

"This is not an appropriate pre-dinner conversation for a young gentleman," Ultra gently chided.

"You're right, Ultra," Harri responded smoothly. "However, I'm glad to hear your dad is moving up in the world, Diego."

The kid snorted. "He had to find a new job because Mom got him fired from one of his old jobs and the other place cut his hours."

Ultra rose from their chair. "Diego, how about you keep the comic your dad gave you, and I'll give you a copy to give to him?"

The kid looked stunned. "Are you kidding? Do you have any idea what your comic is worth?"

"Sweetheart, it's worth far more to me to make a true fan happy." They smiled. "And it sounds like you and your dad are true fans. Come back to my room with me, and I'll sign both with my special pen."

"That would be awesome!" However, the kid's joy flipped to suspicion. "Why do they want me out of the room?" He turned to Harri. "Are you guys going to talk about my dad?"

"Actually, Jeremy and Harri need to talk about a family issue that's not really my business or yours," Ultra said sternly.

"Okay," Diego muttered. "As long as this isn't a bribe."

Ultra placed a manicured hand on their chest. "I would never stoop to bribing a possible future colleague."

Diego followed Ultra out of the living room, chattering about comics the whole way.

Harri turned to Jeremy. "Obviously, Ultra thinks this is important, so spill. Now."

CHAPTER 31

Jeremy seethed at Ultra pushing the issue, but he couldn't get out of it now. Harri resembled a terrier shaking a rat when it came to pursuing secrets. With his suddenly dry mouth, he gulped some of his soda before he began.

"I told you about my encounter with Scorpion Sting and Red Widow, but there was another supervillain encounter no else but Ultra and now Leonardo knew."

"If there's someone else who might hold a grudge against you—" Tim began.

"I didn't tell anyone because it was so fucking embarrassing," Jeremy blurted. "I got picked up by Gentlemen Jim one night fifteen years ago."

Harri stared at him for a long time before she said, "Do you have any idea how lucky you are to be alive?"

She wasn't yelling, but in some ways, this was scarier than when she screamed bloody murder at him.

"Yeah, I do." He shook his head. "You asked me a long time ago what stopped me from picking up guys at clubs. Now, you know the real reason."

"Gentleman Jim isn't just a supervillain," Tim snapped. "He's a psychotic serial killer."

"And he's also a homophobe, Timmy." Jeremy let the sarcasm drip. "He felt me up, and when he found my penis, he planned to kill me for not being—" He made bunny ears with his forefingers. "—a real woman."

"You left that part out, sweetums," Leonardo said as he sat a tray with a cheese ball and crackers on the coffee table.

Jeremy raked his hands through his hair. "I don't like remembering that night, sweetheart. I can usually read a potential partner pretty well. I've only made two big mistakes in my life, and I really resent all of you throwing them in my face."

"I'm not giving you any shit about your taste." Harri reached over and patted his knee. "I just wish you'd told us earlier. I wanted you to keep Nix out of trouble. Not dig yourself into a murder accusation."

"Yeah, what Harri said." Tim smiled. "Take it from me. Those aren't fun."

"If it's any consolation, Tim and Arthur are already keeping tabs on Gentlemen Jim," Harri reached for the spreader and a cracker. "Remember the uninvited guest at our wedding? Somehow, Ted and Jim ended up in a cell together at the Clark County Jail, and now, they're BFFs."

"What?" Her news shook Jeremy out of his own feelings of persecution.

Tim picked up the narrative. "Needless to say, Jim is in Mauvaises, and Ted is in the Clark County Jail. Unless either of them can astral project, I think we can safely rule them out as suspects in Vinh Dang's murder."

Jeremy leaned back in his chair. "Great. We're back to zero suspects, and production starts again tomorrow."

Maybe he should talk with Murph in the morning about the security arrangements and bug Dale Bernhardt about paying for them.

At four-fifty-five the next morning, Mary grumbled under her breath, "I can't believe we have to do this again."

"At least, we're not sneaking around this time." Jeremy kept his eyes closed while she dusted powder over his face. "And I did drive you here and bring you coffee from Java Joe's."

"Sorry, boss," she murmured. "When I'm afraid, I get bitchy. The cops have no clue who killed poor Vinh, we only have rent-a-cops here, and the odds favor one of us as the culprit."

He opened one eye and looked at her. "Is there something you want to confess?"

She grimaced. "You know I don't like using tempered glass files, but I have to admit they'd make a good weapon." She pause as she realized what she just said. "And that's exactly what the killer would tell you, isn't it?"

"Sweetheart, if it's any consolation, I don't think it was you, Phyllis, or Roxanne."

"Let me guess." She smirked as she pulled out a neutral lip color. "You had your sisters run background checks on us?"

"No, I asked the original Ghost Owl to run them."

She froze as she reached for a disposable lip brush. "You knew the original Ghost Owl?"

"He was one of the first supers I designed for. And he's the reason you're the only person besides my husband and my foster sisters who know about my side hustle." He breathed in deeply and exhaled to settle his own jumpiness. "Are you going to give me crap about it like Harri did?"

"No." Mary picked up the brush and dabbed it in the color. "I think you were stupid to associate with a vigilante like him, but I'm sure both Harri and Aisha already told you that. Besides, he's dead now, so it doesn't really matter."

"Yeah." Jeremy blinked away the threatening tears, even though they really were for Harri. "Drowning in Lake Del Oro is a crappy way to die."

When he found out Harri pretended to be the Ghost Owl to stop an attack on Alpha Cola Stadium while Tim was in the hospital, Jeremy had been ready to kill her himself. But thanks to her nearly drowning herself, everyone believed the original Ghost Owl was dead, and Tim had a reason to retire, though it was obvious he resented it at times. But damn, the man turned fifty next month, and he didn't have any super powers. If it weren't for Harri, Tim would have battled himself into an early grave.

"So, is this how it's going to be for the rest of the production?" Mary carefully applied the color to his mouth. "We buddy up like we're in kindergarten again?"

He waited until she was finished with his lips before he declared, "Yes, it is. I don't want to lose you girls or anyone else."

"Not even Renauld Theiss," she teased.

Jeremy snorted. "He's got an ego problem, but that doesn't mean he deserves to die. What's your problem with the man?"

"Our first morning here, he found out three of us work for you. You should have heard the tantrum he threw." Mary lightly dusted Jeremy's mouth with translucent powder. "He screamed at the director before he called Dale Bernhardt and screamed at him."

"And?" Jeremy took the tissue she handed him to blot his lips.

"Renauld didn't get his way." Mary's eyebrow rose. "Then he ran around claiming you were coming on to Vinh right before the police locked us down."

Jeremy said nothing. Mary wasn't a drama queen, but then, he wanted sanity and stability from his employees. Their customers needed a place to relax when they came into the salon, and that was difficult to do with the staff picking fights with each other.

Renauld Thiess's drama queen tendencies were no secret, but was he angry enough about the selection of makeup artists he'd kill Vinh? He had seen Jaye talking to the kid, and Renauld now knew Jaye and Jeremy were the same person. Furthermore, he wasn't happy about not being the head judge in this program.

"I'll keep your warning under advisement," Jeremy said. Like Harri would say, he needed proof before he started making wild accusations.

CHAPTER 32

Once Jeremy's Mister X interviews were done, the director of the show T.K. Julian pulled him aside to talk.

Or rather give Jeremy a lecture from Julian's crossed arms.

"Connie tells me you have some concerns about the judges and contestants."

"I have a concern about how one judge is treating the contestants," Jeremy clarified.

"What?" Julian's eyes narrowed. "You think the Dang kid committed suicide because Theiss said something to him?"

"No, I don't think Vinh committed suicide," Jeremy snapped. "But that doesn't mean another contestant wasn't pushed over the edge and murdered Vinh."

"This is a standard reality show," Julian growled. "All the program participants including yourself signed waivers regarding holding the producers and crew blameless—"

"And Connie made it clear you and the crew would deliberately foster animosity among the contestants." Jeremy shook his head. "Now, there's a dead kid, the police are stumped, and as one of my employees who's subcontracted to the production pointed out, the odds are the murderer is someone connected to the show. Are you going to shrug this off if you're the next target?"

Julian dropped his arms to his sides. "Are you threatening me?"

"We're all in danger, especially since we don't know the motive behind Vinh's murder." Jeremy gestured at the stage. "I hope you and Dale have discussed security measures for the filming with the live audience on Friday. Because that will geometrically increase the victim pool."

The last point seemed to get through to Julian. The cast's waivers would have nothing to do with the production's liability if the producers knew or reasonably suspected one of the cast planned to commit a crime, and they did nothing about it.

Julian nodded slowly. "All right. I get your point. What's your suggestion for the cast and crew in the meantime?"

"We need security cameras everywhere, and no one goes anywhere alone," Jeremy stated. "Those are the directions I gave to my subcontracted staff. My sister has already said the same thing to her clients who are judges and designer contestants."

Julian rubbed his chin. "We already have hidden cameras in the designer's studio across the street. I don't suppose you have a brother who's a tech wizard?"

Jeremy chuckled. "Actually, my brother is an R&B/hip-hop producer. I do have a brother-in-law who handles security for my sisters' law firm."

"All right," Julian said again. "I'll run this by Dale. I apologize for jumping on you, man. If you've got a problem with me in the future, please come to me first." He smiled. "Gossip on a TV set is the same whether you're in Los Angeles or Canyon Pointe."

"I'm sorry for not doing so in the first place. I never thought a random observation might lead to someone's death." Jeremy held out his hand, and they shook on the matter.

Connie reluctantly assigned a private dressing room near the big stage for Jeremy to change. Mary tagged along since Roxanne and Phyllis had gone across the street to take care of the designers and the supers at their makeshift studios.

"Would you please let me help you?" Mary whined.

Jeremy paused in blending his foundation. "Are you telling me I can't do my own makeup?"

"No, I'm telling you I'm bored." She stuck out her tongue.

Maybe it was better to mollify an employee than to remain in such rigid control of his alter ego.

"All right." He held out the makeup sponge. "As long as you understand that if it's not to my liking, you will do it over."

"Yes, Miz Jaye." With a huge grin, Mary jumped off the table she sat on and snatched the sponge before he could change his mind.

When she finished and slipped on the medium-length blond wig, Jaye examined herself in the mirror. "Not bad."

"Not bad for a cis-het girl, you mean?" Mary teased.

"I've been doing my own look for—" Jaye rolled her eyes. "More decades than I'd like to count actually."

The dressing room door opened. "Oops! Sorry!" The door slammed shut before Jaye got a glimpse of the person's face.

"Who was that?" Jaye asked.

"I just saw the person's arm in white cotton with cuffs, but it sounded like a woman's voice," Mary said.

"Did you recognize the voice?"

Mary shook her head.

"Come on." Jaye slipped on her athletic shoes. "I want to make sure they're someone who is allowed in the building."

"Paranoid much, boss?" But Mary followed her to the dressing room door.

Jaye looked over her shoulder. "You didn't spend fifteen minutes trying to revive Vinh." She jerked the door open and listened before she jogged in the direction of what she thought were footsteps. Mary kept pace with her.

A shrill scream came from the opposite direction.

Jaye paused and looked at Mary. She had the same alarmed look Jaye was sure she wore. They pivoted and raced in the direction of the scream. Jaye raced around the corner and was nearly beaned by a flying glass vase. It hit the opposing corridor wall and shattered. Water splashed on the industrial carpet. The orange and yellow arrangement scattered amid the shards and puddle.

A flash of light was followed by the snap, sizzle, and smell of meat frying. Jaye carefully peered around the doorjamb the vase had passed through.

Queen Dazzle danced in a gold, silk dressing robe and her stockinged feet on a chair. A yard away, a cobra smoldered on the floor.

CHAPTER 33

"Jaye! The delivery woman just left!" Queen Dazzle jabbed a finger in the direction Jaye and Mary had just come from.

Jaye tapped the comm in her right earring as she ran down the hallway. "Nix! Where are you?"

"On the big stage. What's going on?"

"Someone delivered a poisonous snake to Dazzle." Jaye pulled ahead of Mary, but only because of her longer legs. The corridor ended and turned in the cross hall that connected the back stage areas of the two theaters.

Nix raced toward them from the opposite end. "Where'd they go?"

Mary patted Jaye's back. "The emergency exit we passed, boss." She started back the way they came.

"But the alarm would have gone off," Jaye protested.

"Unless they were sabotaged." Nix took off after Mary. Jaye didn't have a better idea, so she followed the other two women.

Mary hit the push bar at full speed, Nix on her heels. Alarms blared. Queen Dazzle and security guards came running.

One of the guards had to jog away in order to be heard over the radio. The alarms' obscene noise abruptly cut off.

"What hell is going on?" Murph shouted. "And why is that door open?"

Mary and Nix walked back inside. The superhero walked past the guards and slammed her palm against the drywall. Hard

     Suzan Harden

enough to express her displeasure, but not hard enough to break the plaster.

"If the fake delivery person didn't exit this door, they have to be hiding in the complex," Nix declared.

Murph frowned. "There was a floral delivery van that just left, but those were flowers for Isabella Wang from her husband."

"She must have planned to hide in the room we were using," Mary said.

"She who?" Murph demanded.

Jaye swore. "We need to check on Isabella. Did you get the name of the delivery woman?"

"It wasn't a woman." Murph's face scrunched. "It was a kid, barely out of his teens.

Jaye looked at Queen Dazzle.

The superhero shook her head. "Mine presented as a woman. Latinx. About five-five. She was dressed in a white dress shirt and navy pants with the Fast Floral Delivery Logo on her chest. Dark hair swept up under her cap."

"That sounds like the arm I saw," Mary said.

"Arm?" Murphy looked at the makeup artist.

"Someone started to come into the room Lady Jaye and I were using." Mary shrugged. "I just got a glimpse of a medium brown hand and a white sleeve with a cuff as they pulled the door shut. The person sounded like a woman to me."

"I didn't see the arm," Jaye added. "When the person said 'Oops, sorry,' they sounded like a female to me, too."

"Mr. Murphy, call the police, and tell them Queen Dazzle and I are on the scene," Nix said. "We will help your men sweep the buildings."

Queen Dazzle undid her belt and slid off her robe. Underneath she wore most of her superhero uniform, except she wore athletic slip-ons instead of her gold and green boots.

"Be a dear, Jaye, and hang on to my robe." Dazzle handed the garment to her. "But please don't put it in my dressing room until the odor of lasered snake is cleared from the air."

"Mary and Jaye, stay together and head to the big stage," Nix added. "Tell T.K. that Dazzle and I will be there once we give our statements to the police."

Jaye seethed under her makeup and wig. Nix was young enough to be her daughter.

Queen Dazzle stepped closer and whispered, "I'll keep an eye on her, hun."

Jaye nodded before she stalked off.

Mary followed. "Let's finished getting you dressed before we head to the big stage."

Jaye looked down. She still wore the pale lavender button-down she'd worn as Jeremy and the pair of bicycle shorts to be semi-decent around Mary. She sighed. "You're right."

This was just supposed to be a run-through for Friday night's live filming, but she wanted to wear her shoes she'd selected during the practice runs to make sure she wouldn't fall on her ass while hosting.

The superheroes, the CPPD, and Murph and his team found nothing during their search. Since no one had been injured, the cops took the dead snake and flowers delivered to Queen Dazzle into evidence and wrote up the incident.

Isabella turned out to be safe and sound. Her husband had actually ordered orchids for her. Today was their fortieth anniversary, and he sent a sweet card saying he'd make it up to Isabella when she returned to New York.

With the camera crews capturing the designers actually working in their makeshift studios with the supers they were assigned in the first round, Julian ran Lady Jaye through the judges' introductions. Thank goodness, the words on the teleprompter were large enough Jaye could see them without her reading glasses.

When she introduced Mister X, someone stalked onto the stage. Tall, broad-shouldered, and wearing bulky black clothes and a matching ski mask. But it was the wink that gave Ultramegaperson away. If they were staying with Jaye and Leonardo, what the devil were they doing here?

Jaye's stomach lurched. Dale's assistant Jeff was supposed to pose as Mr. X for the times both Mr. X and Lady Jaye needed to be on stage. Either Ultra talked their boyfriend into having an extra superhero for safety's sake, or Jeff had left the production after Vinh's murder. It was something to look into when Jaye had a chance.

Once Julian was satisfied with their lines and pacing, he dismissed the judges for the day. Before Jaye could approach Mel, they came up to her with Dazzle and Nix in tow.

"Supers meeting in the executive producer's office, sweetheart," they said. "Including you."

Jaye nodded and followed the three superheroes off the stage, but she could feel the eyes of Renauld and Isabella watching them. And she couldn't help wondering if the two other designers were working together to destroy this show and the lives of the people involved.

Chapter 34

When they reached Bernhardt's office, Jaye was surprised to see Tim and Arthur with Dale and Murph. "What's going on?"

"You recommended Mr. Canyon and Mr. Drallhickey to T.K. to provide additional security measures for *Make Me a Superhero*." Bernhardt smiled. "Ultramegaperson and Nix seconded your recommendation rather enthusiastically."

"Actually, it was the D.A. who mentioned the security cameras," Jaye said. "I just passed along his recommendation."

Tim didn't seem surprised by this tidbit. Harri must have informed him of their little talk with Cal. Maybe it technically violated attorney-client privilege, but it was a relief to have Tim here, watching their backs.

Bernhardt abruptly sobered. "Regardless of whose idea it is, something needs to be done. We can't keep going like this. The execs at ABS are nervous about the problems we're having. They gave me a week. If we can't find out who's behind the murder and attempted murder, they're going to shut us down."

Ultra pulled off the ski mask they wore and sat down next to their boyfriend at the little conference table. Their rainbow hair was pinned to their scalp in flat whorls to keep the same silhouette as Jeremy.

"Are you all sure today's incident wasn't a prank?" Tim asked.

"Sugar, I am not Ultramegaperson," Queen Dazzle snapped. "I do not have impenetrable skin. If that cobra had bitten me, I wouldn't be here talking to you right now. Dale's right. It was attempted murder."

"Should we pull in Sparx and Black Falcon to help with security?" Nix suggested.

"Are you saying the three of us can't handle this?" Ultra's right eyebrow rose.

"Every time something has happened, I've been doing shit on stage," Nix snapped. "Maybe you can be in two places simultaneously, but I don't have that power."

"Timmy, what do you need from us?" Jaye interjected before anyone else lost their temper.

"If you, Nix, and Ultra could stick around and help for an hour or two, we can have every nook and cranny of the Jack Canyon under surveillance," Tim answered.

"What about me?" Queen Dazzle scowled at him.

"If you're offering to help, ma'am, I'd be happy to accept any aid you wish to give." Tim smiled.

Jaye watched Arthur. Something was bugging the shy man. He may tell Tim what's bothering him later, but Jaye's instinct said it would be best to get it out in the open now.

"Arthur, you've been very quiet." Jaye gestured to include the entire Jack Canyon Theater complex. "Are you seeing a pattern the rest of us aren't?"

Pink crept up the younger man's face and ears. "Only that I don't believe we are dealing with a supervillain."

"How so?" Tim indicated Arthur to continue.

His Adam's apple bobbed. "Stabbing is very personal and generally indicates great anger or desperation. I cannot see where someone here was desperate enough to protect themselves from Vinh Dang. The method used against Queen Dazzle targeted her at a point in the day when she would in all probability not be wearing her supersuit and therefore be most vulnerable."

"Are you saying my supervillain contestant is innocent?" Bernhardt asked.

Arthur shrugged. "I cannot guarantee such a thing without further investigation, but I calculate the odds to be less than one percent he's guilty."

"Mr. Bernhardt—" Jaye started.

"Please, it's Dale, Lady Jaye." He waved aside the niceties.

"Mr. Julian mentioned there's hidden cameras in the designers' studios," Jaye continued. "Do they run twenty-four-seven?"

Dale shook his head. "They're on motion sensors, so they only film when someone's in one of the studios."

"Good," Tim murmured. "We can confirm the whereabouts of the designers and supers during the time period when the flowers and snake were delivered to Queen Dazzle."

"While you folks deal with the additional cameras, I have other work to attend to." Dale's dismissal was obvious. The kiss he gave Ultramegaperson was a little more circumspect.

Once everyone but Dale was in the hallway, Murph turned to Tim. "Mr. Canyon, may I have a private word with you?"

Jaye noticed Ultra was trying to eavesdrop. She turned to Arthur. "Do you need any assistance with the equipment, Mr. Drallhickey?"

"Please don't treat me any different, Jaye," Arthur murmured. His cheeks were even pinker than before. "Harri says for all intents and purposes, we are family."

"I'm sorry." Jaye smiled. "I was trying to be professional."

Arthur nodded before he turned to their resident snoop. "Ultramegaperson, don't fear for Tim's well-being. Harri has been handling some things for the Murphy family. Please do not pry any further."

"I won't interfere," Ultra murmured. "I met Diego. He's a good kid."

With a bemused smile, Tim walked back to the group while Murph headed in the direction of the security office. "Well, Harri wanted tickets to your first taping. Now, she has them. Let's get the equipment out of the van, and we'll start placing the cameras."

"Don't forget the back hallway between the baby and the big theaters," Jaye said. Something in her said the back hallway was important. The murderer had disappeared in that vicinity twice. If they could find the egress before the bad guy struck again, they had a good chance of catching the jerk.

Chapter 35

At the knock on Harri's office door, she yelled, "Come in!"

As she expected, Susan waltzed into her office, closing the door behind her and wearing a grin that would rival the Cheshire Cat's.

"Your delivery to Special Agent Consuelo went well I take it?" Harri asked.

"Even better than you and Tim planned." Susan sat in one of the visitor chairs. "Nesmith was at her office. They're planning to use the new materials to lure their suspected NSB mole out of his hole."

There was more to the story from Susan's delight. Harri sat back in her office chair and waited. Finally, her partner's pleased expression faded.

"Remind me to never play poker with you," Susan grumbled. Harri smirked.

"They wanted to know who you suspected was behind the super disappearances fifty-plus years ago."

Harri straightened and blurted, "What did you tell them?"

"I told them the truth," Susan said dryly.

Harri scowled at her partner. Not even Aisha was this evil with her news.

"I told them you were clueless." Susan waved her hand. "They asked if I knew and I said I had a prime suspect, but I want to hear their theory before I gave them mine."

"Please tell me they're on the right track," Harri said.

"They are." Susan shrugged. "They're divided though. Wilbur

thinks you're too sentimental, which is why you don't suspect Rue Liberty. Sylvia believes you do know. And you finagled Nix into loft-sitting for Aisha and Rey, so you could feed false info to Rue Liberty."

"Wow," Harri murmured. "So, I'm either too stupid to live, or I'm the smartest supervillain alive."

"They did let one thing slip," Susan added. "The bullets from Miss Purrception's hideout and the ones Serena pulled out of her torso are from the same military shipment that was stolen five years ago. They aren't sure if Corvus stole it for themselves, Corvus stole it for Rue Liberty, or Rue raided Corvus depots before the feds could get to them."

"I wouldn't be surprised if it were option number four," Harri said dryly. "There's Corvus depots the feds didn't find."

The intercom buzzed. Harri tapped the button. "Yes?"

"Your hubby's on line two," Janna reported.

"Send him through." When the designated line blinked, Harri hit the button and placed the call on speaker. "Hey, honey, what's up?"

"You called it," Tim said. "The attempt this time was on Queen Dazzle. Our culprit delivered a cobra to her."

"She's fine though, right?" Harri asked.

"She's fine. Bernhardt hired Canyon and Company on the spot, so Arthur and I will be here for a little while." Tim sighed. "I know it means more overtime for Dajon—"

"That man is worth every penny," Harri retorted. "But if he has plans for tonight, I'll watch Grace until Patty gets home from classes."

"Yes, I know how tortured you are watching your goddaughter." Tim laughed. "Also, Carl Murphy gave me two tickets to the Friday live taping. He asked if you would bring Diego."

"Of course, I will." Harri fist-pumped the air. She'd been

trying to get tickets for the last several weeks, but the legit sales places were incredibly expensive for the handful of seats left. And forget about the scalpers' prices.

"Want some good news?" Harri said.

"Sure."

"Tweedle Dee and Tweedle Dum have finally put yours and Susan's puzzle pieces together."

"So Consuelo finally brought in Nesmith." Tim whistled. "Took them long enough."

"Compared to you, Mr. Genius?" Susan blurted.

"You put me on speaker phone so your partner can mess with me?" One could almost hear Tim's eyes roll. "I cannot wait until Aisha is back from France. You two feed off each other's worst vices."

"Hey!" Harri and Susan protested at the same time.

Tim laughed. "See you when I get home. Love you, honey."

"I love you, too, Tim," Susan mocked.

Harri laughed and shook her head. "Me, too!"

She hated to admit it, but Susan's news was a relief. The sooner the feds arrested Rue Liberty, the sooner she could get Miss Purr-ception out of the Lechuza Building.

CHAPTER 36

Jeremy blessed the stars that the rest of the week went by smoothly. Tim and Arthur kept surveillance on the Jack Canyon Theater going around the clock, both with the on-site security guards and them keeping an eye on their cameras personally. However, nothing unusual appeared on the video.

On Friday night, the show's assistant director Connie Bancroft kept the supers together. They wore huge, hooded black cloaks with black veils over their faces. Only their respective designers knew what each super wore beneath the thick billowy material.

Crew raced back and forth, double checking all connections between the digital recorders, sound, and cameras. By herself in a corner, Lady Jaye practiced her breathing exercises. Tonight, her first outfit consisted of black trousers, a matching tuxedo jacket, and a white high-collared shirt with a cloth-of-gold vest and bow-tie. Her black oxfords were comfortable to walk on the stage. With her nerves, she worried about a pratfall during the taping.

It wasn't like she hadn't done this almost every weekend at Lady Jaye's Revue. The only difference was there'd never been a murderer running around at the Revue.

That she knew of.

"And now, our hostess, Canyon Pointe's very own Lady Jaye!" the program announcer thundered.

The intro music played, and she strode out onto the stage to exuberant applause.

"Thank you!" She waved both hands to the audience she

couldn't see through the spotlight. "Thank you, my lovelies! Welcome to the first round of judging for *Make Me a Superhero!*"

The crowd roared its approval.

"First up, let's meet our judges." Jaye whipped through the introductions. Each of the four judges and the Mr. X decoy walked out onto the stage and said a few words before they took their seats on Jaye's right.

"Our first design contestant tonight is a student from UCLA—"

A scream ripped through the air followed by someone shouting, "Gun!"

Someone in the lighting booth cut the stage lights and the spotlight before bringing up the house lights. Audience members panicked and stampeded up the aisles.

Jaye's heart attempted to jump out of her throat and run away. In the front row, Harri tried to shield Diego from a petite woman aiming a handgun at them.

CHAPTER 37

Jaye took a step forward, but Queen Dazzle yanked her back.

"Put the gun down, Isla," Harri said. "You don't want Diego to see this."

"You took him from me!" the woman who must be the kid's biological mother shrieked. "You conspired with that no-good worthless jerk of a husband to take my son from me!"

"Don't be a fool, Isla." Harri shook her head. "Judge Shriver will never let you have custody again if you don't put down the gun."

"I don't care!" Isla Murphy screamed.

While Harri tried to talk Diego's mother down, security cleared the stage of everyone except the three supers and Jaye. And she damn well wasn't leaving until she knew her sister and Harri's foster son were okay.

Murph walked into the theater, unarmed. He didn't have the nightstick or the taser the security guards normally carried.

"Isla, put down the gun," he said gently. "We lost custody of Diego because of our own stupidity."

"Not until that bitch gives him back!"

"You're Diego's mom, right?" Nix slowly descended the steps on the right of the stage. "Take me instead. My mom abandoned me and my sister. I would love to have a mom like you."

Ultramegaperson was already flying straight for Harri and Diego when Isla whirled to face Nix. She pulled the trigger, but Nix was already somersaulting out of the line of fire. Ultra flew Harri and the kid out of the theater's main exits.

Isla screamed in fury and turned toward the next closet target. Jaye didn't see her life flash before her eyes. All she saw was Leonardo's face in her mind.

Before someone slammed her to the hardwood planking of the stage.

"Isla, no!"

Jaye peeked under Queen Dazzle's elbow to see Murph rush his ex-wife. The pair struggled for the gun. There was a loud pop. The pair separated. Isla still had the gun.

Dazzle rolled off Jaye, took aim with her finger, and shot a laser beam at the firearm. Unfortunately, she hit the removable clip. The overheated bullets exploded.

This time, Isla's scream was one of pain at her ruined hand. She and Murph dropped to the floor at the same time.

Nix radioed the CPPD that the gunman was down.

Jaye rushed down to Murph, pulling off her jacket on the way. She knelt next to him and attempted to staunch the blood spurting from the hole in his chest.

"J-Jaye," Murph wheezed. "T-tell D-Diego . . ." He struggled to breathe to get the words out. "T-tell him . . ."

"You're going to tell him you love him and you're proud of him yourself," Jaye assured Murph. "Save your strength to tell him and hug him."

When the paramedics raced in a couple of minutes later, she knew it was already too late.

CHAPTER 38

Saturday morning, Jeremy dragged himself out of bed and into the kitchen. Every muscle and joint ached from Queen Dazzle pushing him down on the stage floor last night when Isla Murphy started shooting. Two boxes of pastries sat on the breakfast bar. The bake shop down the street was Leonardo's refuge when stressed. Jeremy couldn't blame his love.

But worse than the sweet morsels tempting him was the voice of Essie Morales. He sauntered over to the living area to find his husband and their guests watching the twenty-four-hour Action 12! News channel.

. . . Lady Jaye's attorney Harri Winters had this to say earlier this morning."

The scene switched from the studio to Harri and all of the Canyon Pointe queens outside of the Revue. "Lady Jaye and the staff and performers of the Revue send their condolences to Carl Murphy's family. In the short time Lady Jaye knew Mr. Murphy, she found him to be an intelligent, thoughtful, and kind friend as well as an excellent coworker. He will be missed."

The screen flashed back to the studio. "Again, if you're just tuning in, a shooter opened fire on the Jack Canyon Theater main stage last night during the recording of the TV program, *Make Me a Superhero*—"

"Darling, would you please shut that noise off?" Jeremy said.

Leonardo pressed the button on the remote. "I'm sorry. I didn't realize you were awake. How are you feeling?"

"Like shit," Jeremy grumbled as he sat beside his husband on the couch.

"The good news is with the publicity, we got the greenlight from the network to finish filming the show," Dale said brightly.

"Yippee." Jeremy glared at the producer.

"Oh, Jaye, honey." Mel shook their head. "You can't blame yourself for what happened."

"We had three supers and a dozen wannabes on hand, and a man still died."

Mel rose from the loveseat where they sat with Dale to sit on Jeremy's other side. "And sometimes, all the powers in the world don't mean squat. Aisha told me that years ago, babydoll." They patted Jeremy's leg.

"Tell that to Murph's kid," Jeremy said morosely.

Two days later, Jeremy and Leonardo went to Carl Murphy's funeral. There wasn't much family there, but the man had a lot of friends. Somehow, poor Diego kept his composure through the whole ceremony, even when he spoke a few words on his father's behalf.

Harri rented out Nolan's for the entire afternoon so the family and friends could drink and talk. When Diego slipped out of the banquet room, Jeremy told Leonardo he'd be right back and followed the teen out to the patio. Diego perched on the half-wall at an angle where no one could see him from the restaurant's window.

Jeremy sat next to him but remained quiet.

After five minutes, Diego said, "Aren't you going to give me the lecture about how things will get better?"

"Nope." Jeremy eyed the teen. "You're the only one who can decide whether things are better."

Diego closed his eyes and leaned against the building. "Maybe, in a way, things are better. My parents won't be fighting over me any more."

"Yeah, but most parents don't bring a gun to a custody battle."

Diego snorted. "True." He opened his eyes and looked at Jeremy. "Harri said you and she were the same age as me when you both lost your dads."

Jeremy nodded. "We were, but we did find new family."

Diego gave a little half-smile. "I think I did, too." He reached over and hugged Jeremy.

And for the first time in a very long time, Jeremy felt something loosen inside of himself. He released his old anger at his own parents and let it drift away.

He could only hope that maybe, someday, Diego could do the same with his.

Turn the page to read an excerpt from the next volume,

A Very Hero Terror!

A VERY HERO TERROR

Nevada State Penitentiary, a week ago

"Wakey, wakey, Teddy Bear."

Ted Meadowfield jerked upright at the sing-song voice and banged his head on the metal frame of his bunkbed. "Ow! What the hell—"

Someone placed a finger across Ted's lips, and he stopped speaking. A dark figure crouched next to his bunk. Recognition chilled and warmed him at the same time.

Gentleman Jim's filed teeth glinted under the lamplight from the prison block's hallway.

"How did you—?" Ted kept his voice low.

"I waited until the guys with sticks up their butts believed you and I would be good little boys," the supervillain whispered. "Now, we can go have some fun."

"What about—" Ted pointed at the bunk above him.

"I'm sorry." Jim smiled. "I started having fun without you. I won't do it again."

Something warm dripped onto Ted's hand. It was too thick to be his cellmate's drool or urine. He swallowed hard and tried to ignore the second drip.

He thought gaining Gentleman Jim's confidence and writing an exposé of the supervillain would put him back on the news map. His agent had launched an auction between the three biggest publishers in New York yesterday.

"Jim, if we both escape at the same time, the authorities won't stop until they find us."

"Have you changed your mind about taking your revenge on that Winters bitch?"

God, it was so tempting. Jim knew the art of inflicting pain. Ted could learn so much from the supervillain. He wanted to learn. He needed Harri Winters to pay for what she did to him. That bitch had destroyed his career. Thanks to her, his wife left him. Not even his kids would talk to him anymore.

Ted nodded. "All right. Let's go." He wiped his hand off on his pillow and flipped it so the guards wouldn't see the blood.

Jim rose and stepped out of Ted's way as he swung his feet off the bed. He donned the canvas slip-ons he'd been given when he arrived at the state pen. A few flicks of his bedding made it look like he was still asleep. The guards would ignore him, like they always did, until morning roll call.

"Come on." Jim checked the hallway before he slipped out of the open cell door.

"Wait." Ted rearranged his cellmate's covers so they absorbed and hid the blood still flowing from the other man's neck. Then he grabbed his notebook and Jim's letters and stepped into the hallway.

"Why do you need those?" Jim hissed.

"I'm not taking the chance the authorities break your code," Ted whispered.

His excuse seemed to satisfy the supervillain. Together, they left the cell block. By the time they reached the staff parking lot, Jim jingled the warden's keys in synch with the tune he whistled.

And Ted tried not to think about the bodies Gentleman Jim left in their wake.

ACKNOWLEDGEMENTS

I can't say enough wonderful things about my cover artist Elaina Lee and my formatter J.W. Manus. They go above and beyond no matter what stupid thing I do or say.

To my cohorts, Tracie, Candi, and Kate, thanks for all your encouragement through the pandemic. You three are the writerly balm that sooths my soul.

To my good friends, Angie and Jo, thank you for listening to me during last year's trials and tribulations. You kept me from falling apart.

And much love and laughter to Darling Husband, Genius Kid, and Princess Bella. You three make my world complete.

About the Author

Suzan Harden transitioned from writing information technology manuals for companies and legal articles for a law enforcement magazine to her first love, fantasy and science fiction in all their forms. She's the author of the Bloodlines, the 888-555-HERO, and the Justice series.

www.ingramcontent.com/pod-product-compliance
Lightning Source LLC
Chambersburg PA
CBHW071529120726
47907CB00013B/1266